This book belongs to

_____

_____

_____

ALEX AND PENNY IN THE WILD WEST

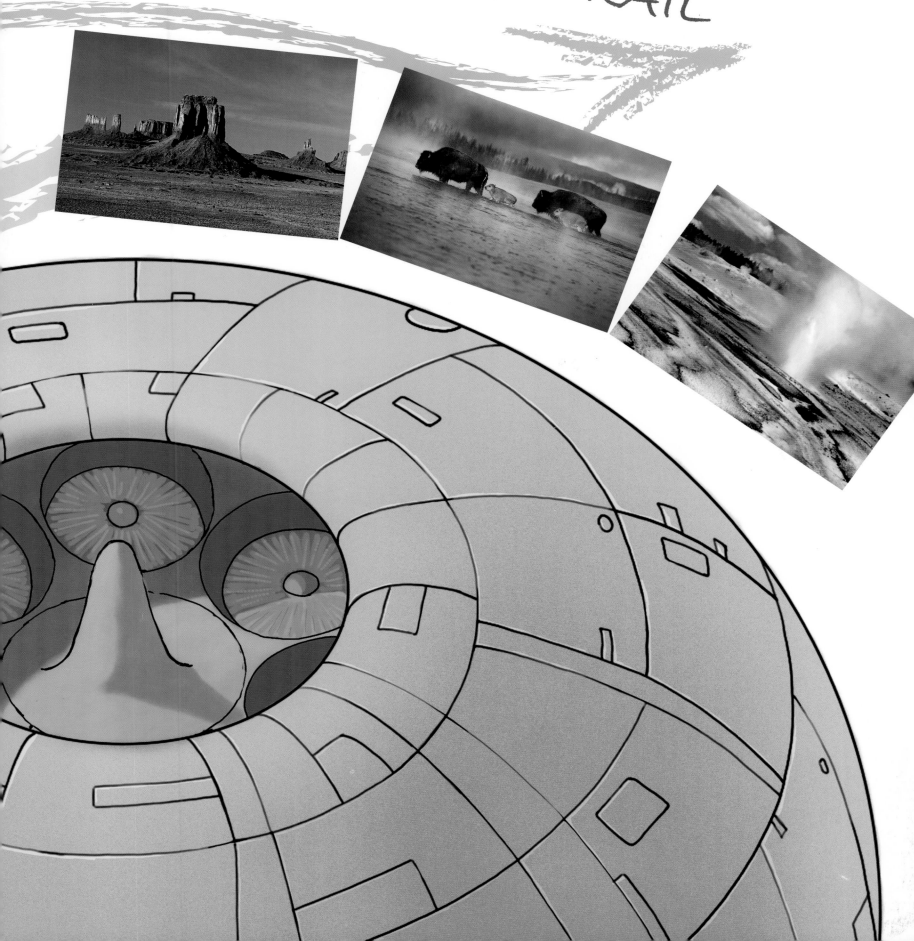

THE MAIN CHARACTERS OF THIS STORY ARE: ALEX AND PENNY

Hi! I'm Penny, Alex's sister. We're twins, but we don't resemble each other at all. To start with, I'm older than him… by five minutes! I love drawing and want to be a famous painter when I grow up. Alex calls me "Miss Know-It-All" and says that I'm the smart aleck of the family, but the truth is that I adore reading books, stories and comics. However, there are plenty of things that I don't know – for example, I'm hopeless at math!

What do you like?
Write to my e-mail address to tell me all about yourself:

penny@whitestar.it

I'm Alex, Penny's brother. They say I'm a computer whiz…. Actually, without meaning to boast, I'm much more than that: an Internet genius, a videogame wizard and the world gaming champion! Unlike that know-it-all sister of mine, they say that I'm always in trouble and that if I can't find any, I invent some. It's just that I'm adventurous, really!

What about you?
Write to my e-mail address to tell me all about yourself:

alex@whitestar.it

EPSILON AND ITS
INVENTOR, KAPPA

WS SPECIAL
AGENTS!

MISTERIUS

It all started when we read a very strange
announcement in the newspaper: "Seeking agents
willing to deal with risks and danger; great smartness
and cunning required." How could we resist the
temptation? When we answered we met Kappa, who's
a brilliant inventor (though absolutely hopeless at
disguises).... Kappa explained that in order to take part
in the adventures promised in the announcement, we'd
have to prove our courage and smartness by trying to
discover what was hidden behind the mysterious
WS agency! We thus set off for an adventure
in the skies above Italy, aboard Epsilon, a super-
technological hot-air balloon, discovering curious
facts about the country's most famous monuments.
We followed the clues to the WS headquarters,
where we met Cornelius Misterius, the director-general
of the World Secret Investigation Agency, which
investigates unsolved mysteries all over the world.
And that's how we became special agents! Who
knows what our next adventure will be?

"Bang … Bang! Bang!"

"Hey, Alex! Turn the volume down, I'm trying to read!"

"Little sister, you are always trying to read. All that reading is bad for your eyes!"

"And your video games are good for you, aren't they, Alex?"

"First of all Penny, this is not just 'a' video game, it is 'the' video game! 'Wild West 3' is a fantastic game. I am Kidd Boy, and I am fighting in a gun duel with the fearsome bandit Jack Carson."

"And blah blah blah… it is just a video game."

"It isn't, Penny! Look at the graphics, it feels like being in the Wild West. You have a go! You will breathe the dust from the streets, you will hear the music from the saloon, it will seem like you can see the Indians' arrows flying and…"

"WATCH OUT!"

Alex lowered his head instinctively, just in time to avoid an Indian arrow!

"An Indian arrow? Now we are exaggerating with virtual reality!" Alex stared in amazement at the arrow, which, thanks to a sucker, had stuck to the computer screen. "This video game is great! The special effects are fantastic!!"

Penny, who did not believe that the arrow had come from the video game, got up to move towards the window where she had caught sight of a suspicious-looking feather.

"Little brother, come and see who shot the arrow! It looks like a very special Indian has come to see us."

"Kappa!" Alex ran to greet the young inventor from the World Secret Agency, who had become their friend since their first adventure as special WS agents. As usual the ingenious inventor, who was completely hopeless at disguises, had chosen a very strange outfit.

"Kappa, why are you dressed as an Indian?"

The answer left the twins speechless. "So that I'm ready for your next adventure! You are just about to go to the Wild West!"

"Kappa," butted in Penny as she recalled the many things she had read on the subject. "It's impossible! The Wild West is really a historical period, not a place."

"Not even Epsilon can take us to the old Wild West!" exclaimed Alex with a hint of disappointment in his voice. "It would have to take us back a couple of centuries!"

"That's just what we intend to do!"

"WHAT?" The twins looked at each other in amazement. "Do you want us to travel in time?"

"That's the idea. General Manager Misterius has asked me to think of a way to take you back to the time when the

West was discovered, and I think I have succeeded! Actually it wasn't an easy task at all. It took me several days to work out how to polarize the valves so that the electron beam coming from the cathode reversed the magnetic field increasing...."

"Wait a minute!" interrupted Penny in exasperation. "We can't understand a word of what you're saying! What are you talking about?"

"About this!" exclaimed Kappa, moving the canvas sheet that covered Penny's desk, revealing....

"Granddad's old radio! The one I gave you a month ago to mend! You've taken it to bits!"

"No, I've repaired it. The radio is working perfectly, but now it is also a bipolar device for traveling through time!"

"Wow! Kappa, you're a genius!"

"I wonder if Granddad will agree, little brother? Kappa, can you tell us why we should go to the Wild West."

"I won't do it, but Misterius will. He will connect with you on Epsilon's computer. Come, let's go into the garden. I have parked the hot-air balloon behind the house."

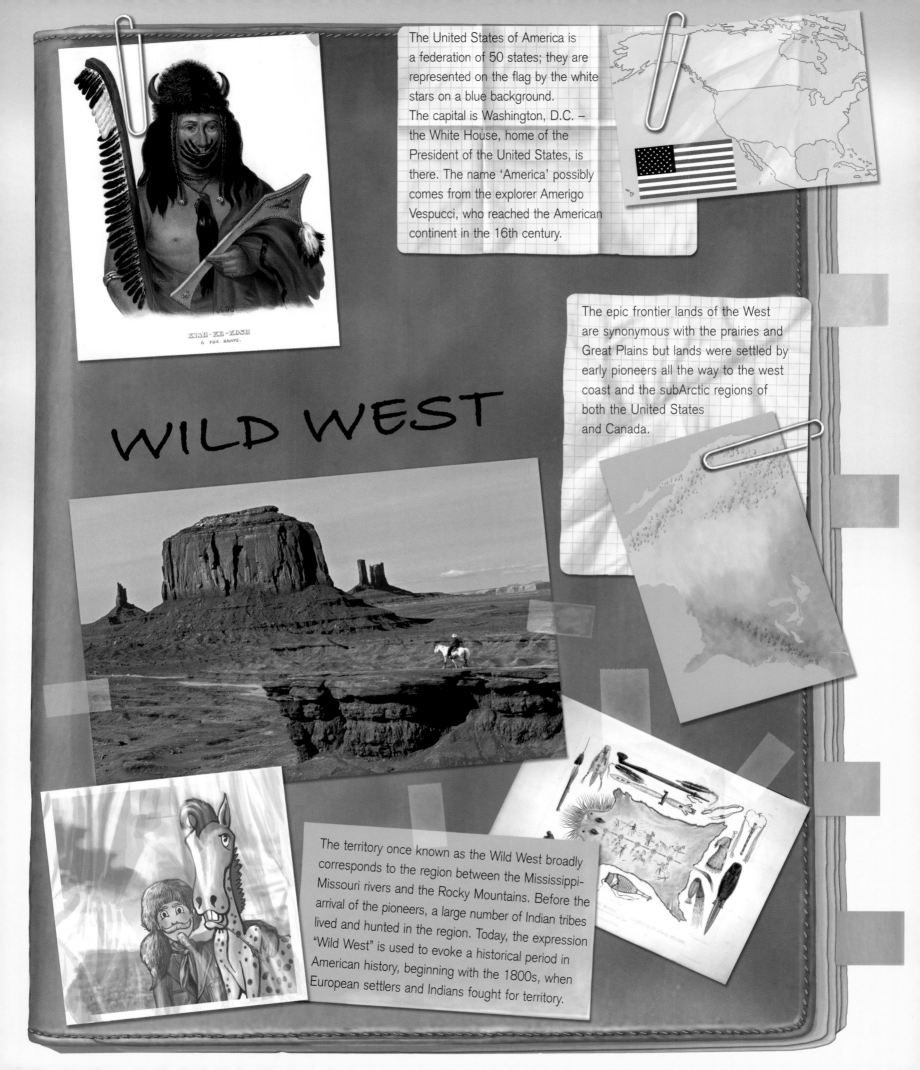

KISH-KE-KOSH
A FOX BRAVE.

WILD WEST

The United States of America is a federation of 50 states; they are represented on the flag by the white stars on a blue background. The capital is Washington, D.C. – the White House, home of the President of the United States, is there. The name 'America' possibly comes from the explorer Amerigo Vespucci, who reached the American continent in the 16th century.

The epic frontier lands of the West are synonymous with the prairies and Great Plains but lands were settled by early pioneers all the way to the west coast and the subArctic regions of both the United States and Canada.

The territory once known as the Wild West broadly corresponds to the region between the Mississippi-Missouri rivers and the Rocky Mountains. Before the arrival of the pioneers, a large number of Indian tribes lived and hunted in the region. Today, the expression "Wild West" is used to evoke a historical period in American history, beginning with the 1800s, when European settlers and Indians fought for territory.

"Good morning special agents!"

"Good morning, Misterius!" replied the twins in unison.

"I believe that agent Kappa has already told you what I am about to ask you."

"We already know Misterius!" interrupted Alex. "You want to suggest a journey in time going back to the Wild West, and our answer in yeeeeeeeeees!"

"But first we would like to know what our mission is going to be," added Penny, in a down-to-earth way.

"Now I'll explain: what Kappa is going to give you is my great-great-uncle MacKenzie Misterius' diary, which I came across, er... let's say by chance... rm... in our archives."

"But boss, I thought that you had found it when you were cleaning out the cellar!"

"Erm... Yes Agent Kappa, but it's not important where it was found whereas, more to the point, what is written in it. You should know that my great-great-uncle was one of the first general managers of the World Secret Agency and, as such, explored the so-called Wild West for several months. At the time, there was no greater mystery to uncover: the territories to the west of the Mississippi River, at the beginning of the 19th century were, in fact, unexplored. It was known that there were immense plains inhabited by Indian tribes, but, much as it may seem strange to us today, until two centuries ago, nobody else, apart from the Indians, had crossed the territory of the United States of America. MacKenzie Misterius kept a gripping diary that tells of all his discoveries and adventures, but, in particular, his second journey contains a reference to something very mysterious – the very powerful Mic-Ko-Suc."

"The what?"

"Mic-Ko-Suc, Alex. It is what my great-great-uncle calls something he describes as the most powerful and sacred Indian secret."

"And he doesn't explain what it is?"

"No, Penny. Unfortunately the last pages of the diary are missing. I have searched for references to this mysterious Indian secret but there is no trace in the agency archives. I have also tried to reconstruct my forefather's journey but, unfortunately, my great-great-uncle loved secret codes and cryptography. The name of each destination is hidden in a quiz or puzzle that you have to solve before you can go on. That is why you have to take the diary with you. It will be very useful to you for important information on the Wild West, and it is indispensable for going ahead with the mission. Now, though, enough talking. Twins, are you ready to leave on your new mission?"

"YEEEEEEEEEES!"

"Have a good journey then, and be careful!"

THE MISSISSIPPI and THE MISSOURI RIVERS

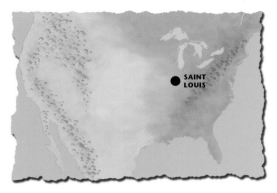

SAINT LOUIS

"WOW! What a trip! It felt like being inside a washing machine, but not quite! It was more like being inside a blender! It was incredible, wasn't it Alex? Little brother? Are you all right? You look a bit green."

"I'm fine!" mumbled Alex, even though the expression on his face seemed to say exactly the opposite.

"Don't worry, Alex. It's just a simple matter of time sickness."

"KAPPA!" exclaimed the twins in chorus, rushing to the on-board computer from which the voice of their inventor friend was coming.

"I'm glad to see that you have come out of the time tunnel unhurt. I wasn't quite sure that I had made all the necessary adjustments to your Granddad's radio."

"Maybe that's why I can feel my stomach close to my ears!" exclaimed Alex crossly.

14

"Well... thinking about it... Yes, it is possible that that is the reason for it, but don't worry Alex, your stomach will soon be back to normal. Meanwhile, I have to plot your position on the World Secret central computer, so look around and tell me what you can see."

Penny leaned out of the hot-air balloon to observe the place they were flying over:

"I can see a big river, two in fact! It seems that we are flying over the point where two huge rivers meet! Where are we Kappa?"

"At the exact spot where MacKenzie Misterius started his journey! My calculations were exactly right! I had serious doubts about that ionic condenser...."

"Kappa!"

A steam boat used by the settlers to go upstream.

"Oh... sorry Penny... to answer your question: you are flying over the area where the Missouri and Mississippi rivers meet, the two largest rivers in North America. In a few minutes time you will whiz over the city of St. Louis, from where the steamboats used by many settlers left to reach what will also be your first destination: Independence. This little town became famous because it was the departure point for the long and dangerous journey to the West! What do you say, guys – do you want to visit a real frontier town?"

"Anything, as long as we can get out of Epsilon... I'm not feeling too well."

"Come on Alex! Our great adventure in the West is just beginning. And to start in the best possible way, please, little brother, try not to be sick on the sheriff!"

The Mississippi is the longest river in North America. Its waters form the boundaries of six States!

The Missouri River has its source in the Rocky Mountains and joins the Mississippi 2314 miles downstream.

DID YOU KNOW?

The first people to explore the "Wild West" were not the settlers. In May 1804, the President of the United States Thomas Jefferson gave two army officers, Lewis and Clark, the task of finding a waterway linking the west and east coasts of the continent. The two explorers left from St. Louis and went upstream along the Missouri for miles in a canoe. After countless adventures the expedition reached its objective – the Pacific Ocean. It was November 7th, 1805.

LEWIS AND CLARK

WELCOME TO INDEPENDENCE

In the streets of Independence, in spring, there is a festive atmosphere as the moment of departure draws near. The settlers are very busy repairing their wagons and making their last purchases before the wagon train sets off. Independence was also a lucky city from another point of view, and enjoyed a very different from that of other towns in the West. How would you like to live in Tombstone for example? Or in Deadwood or Town Without Pity? How would you like to explore a typical frontier town? Explore it with us using the drawing and notes in MacKenzie Misterius' diary as a map.

SALOON

The bar of the West. Go through its creaking swinging doors and walk up to the bar. I would strongly advise you not to order a whiskey, which is made of pure alcohol, chewing tobacco and a little sugar (which is certainly not enough to sweeten it). But if you wish, you can take the risk and order it all the same, using the names by which it is known around here: tarantula juice, red eye, casket varnish or fire water. Poker is played at the tables. Be careful: many of the players are professional cheats who spend their days hoping to find a sitting duck.

DRUGSTORE

You can find anything you need in this store, from utensils to clothes, from a horse harness to coffee. Here you will also be able to sample the cakes and biscuits made by the lady who owns or runs the drugstore.

BANK

Banks are very widespread in the West as the traveling pioneers need to have access to money for any purchases they may need to make. Opening a bank, furthermore, is not particularly difficult and success is guaranteed. But if you are thinking of going into this business, don't forget that bank robberies are an everyday event!

THE DOCTOR'S HOUSE

You don't think you're going to find a hospital in a frontier town, do you? There may be a doctor if you're lucky... well... maybe some people wouldn't call it luck – you just have to remember that, in these times, the instrument most used by doctors was the saw because amputation was the only sure way to stop the spread of an infection!

THE SHERIFF'S OFFICE

DO YOU WANT TO KNOW EVERYTHING ABOUT THE GUARDIANS OF THE LAW IN THE WEST? TURN THE PAGE!

SHERIFF'S...

First of all, forget the sheriffs you've seen in westerns, always busy chasing gangs of bandits and always on the side of justice! The truth was slightly different! Life in the West was not regimented by strict official laws like those that regulated the east of the United States, because the problems were decisively different. For example, in New York, capital punishment was an absurd consequence for somebody who stole a horse, but in the arid expanses of the West, where a person's life depended on horses, such punishment did not seem so strange! The guardians of the Law therefore found themselves applying a code

of behavior that was dictated by confrontation with daily life, rather than by a written rule. It goes without saying that the boundary between what was allowed and what was not had become rather fine, and while some judges and sheriffs lost their lives defending justice, others did not have any qualms about reconciling their own role with that of the outlaw. This was the case of Henry Plummer: he became famous precisely because he successfully integrated his career as a sheriff with that of a bandit.

WOULD YOU PREFER TO WEAR THE SHINING SHERIFF'S STAR OR TO IMPERSONATE A CLEVER BANK ROBBER?
CHOOSE THE ROLE YOU WISH TO PLAY, AND SELECT THE GAME TO PLAY ACCORDINGLY – OR, IF YOU PREFER, TRY TO GET INTO BOTH ROLES AND FIND OUT WHAT YOUR TRUE VOCATION IS!

ARE YOU THE SHERIFF? JUMP ON YOUR HORSE AND SET OFF AT A GALLOP TO CHASE THE GANG OF ROBBERS. ONLY ONE OF THE ROADS WILL GET YOU TO THE BANDITS BEFORE THEY DISAPPEAR UNDERGROUND TO THEIR SECRET HIDEOUT!

...BANDITS

If sheriffs were not all champions of the Law as you might have expected, then we should also dispel another myth: not all bandits were murderers without principles who were able to organize brilliant robberies and make off with the booty. Some were regarded as gentlemen and others organized the worst robberies ever seen in history. Here are their exploits.

The most unfortunate robbery in history, was organized by the Dalton brothers. Wanted after robbing a train, five members of the Dalton gang had the marvelous idea of ending their criminal careers with a final bang, which, had it been successful, would have allowed them to live comfortably enjoying the money from the plunder and enormous popularity. The plan, in fact, was to rob two banks in the same town at the same time – something that nobody had previously succeeded in doing. Unfortunately, even the Daltons did not succeed as they were recognized by a passer-by as they went into the bank, despite their clever disguises that included wigs and false beards! The robbery ended before it began with a shoot-out that killed all five reckless thieves.

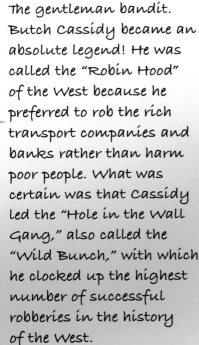

REWARD
($5,000.00)
Reward for the capture, dead or alive, of one Wm. Wright, better known as

"BILLY THE KID"

Age, 18. Height, 8 feet, 3 inches. Weight, 125 lbs. Light hair, blue eyes and even features. He is the leader of the worst band of desperadoes the Territory has ever had to deal with. The above reward will be paid for his capture or positive proof of his death.
JIM DALTON, Sheriff

DEAD OR ALIVE!
"BILLY THE KID"

The gentleman bandit. Butch Cassidy became an absolute legend! He was called the "Robin Hood" of the West because he preferred to rob the rich transport companies and banks rather than harm poor people. What was certain was that Cassidy led the "Hole in the Wall Gang," also called the "Wild Bunch," with which he clocked up the highest number of successful robberies in the history of the West.

19

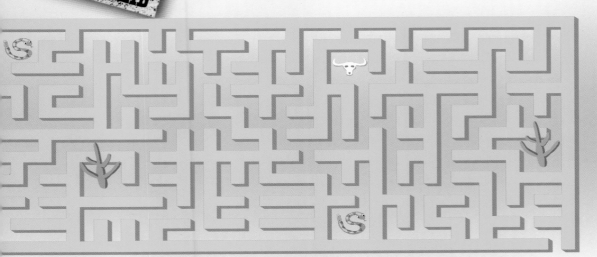

ARE YOU THE CUNNING BANDIT? YOU WILL NEED THE COMBINATION TO OPEN THE SAFE! THE BANK MANAGER HAS BEEN SMART: HE HAS HIDDEN THE SEQUENCE IN A MATHEMATICAL GAME. TO FIND THE COMBINATION, WORK OUT THE FOLLOWING MATHEMATICAL EQUATIONS BY REPLACING THE SYMBOLS WITH THE CORRECT NUMBERS.

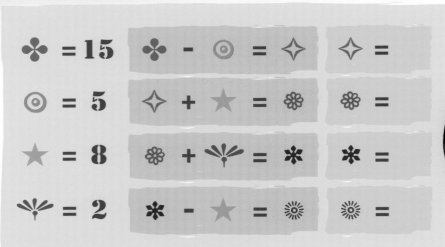

$$\clubsuit = 15$$
$$\odot = 5$$
$$\star = 8$$
$$\psi = 2$$

$$\clubsuit - \odot = \diamondsuit \qquad \diamondsuit =$$
$$\diamondsuit + \star = \circledast \qquad \circledast =$$
$$\circledast + \psi = \ast \qquad \ast =$$
$$\ast - \star = \circledcirc \qquad \circledcirc =$$

OREGON TRAIL

Spring has arrived in Independence, and the moment of departure is drawing near. In fact, the settlers have waited for the grass to grow long enough so as to guarantee nourishment for the oxen that will pull the wagons along the entire trip to the West. The town is now so crowded that it takes you a whole day to reach your friends' or relatives' wagons. In the meantime, the last purchases have been made and, most importantly, the route that the caravan will take is studied: the Oregon Trail. The Oregon Trail was, in reality, much more than a simple trail. Since 1843, the year in which the real "conquest" of the West began, it was just about the only way to cross the territories of the West. Half a million pioneers heading for California faced this long and dangerous 2000-mile, six-month journey, enduring incredible difficulties and suffering.

A day in the life of a pioneer!

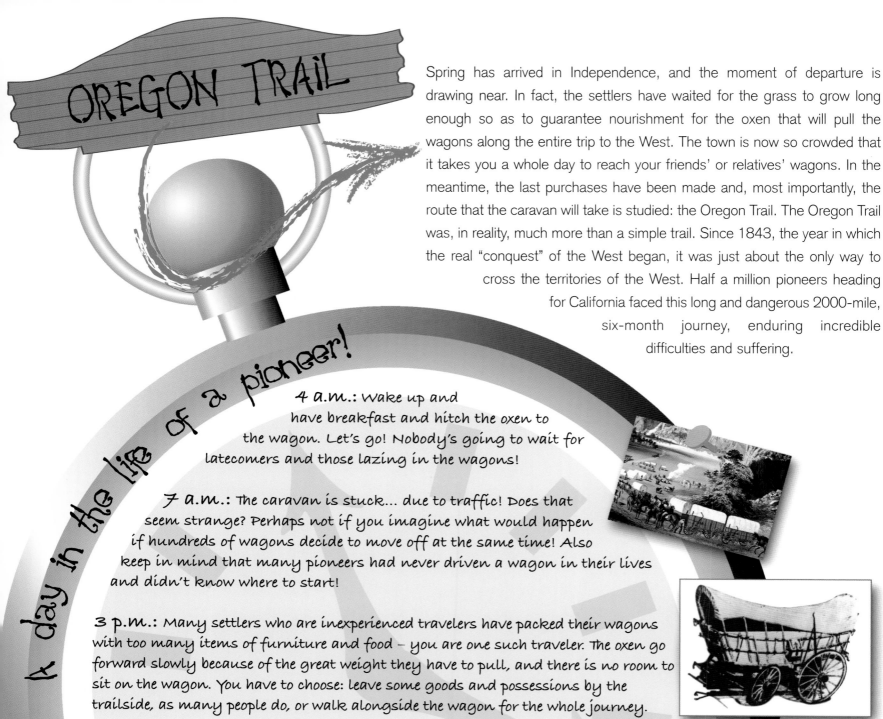

4 a.m.: Wake up and have breakfast and hitch the oxen to the wagon. Let's go! Nobody's going to wait for latecomers and those lazing in the wagons!

7 a.m.: The caravan is stuck… due to traffic! Does that seem strange? Perhaps not if you imagine what would happen if hundreds of wagons decide to move off at the same time! Also keep in mind that many pioneers had never driven a wagon in their lives and didn't know where to start!

3 p.m.: Many settlers who are inexperienced travelers have packed their wagons with too many items of furniture and food – you are one such traveler. The oxen go forward slowly because of the great weight they have to pull, and there is no room to sit on the wagon. You have to choose: leave some goods and possessions by the trailside, as many people do, or walk alongside the wagon for the whole journey.

6 p.m.: At last you stop for the night. The pioneers arrange the wagons in a circle for safety from the Indians. To tell the truth, you needn't worry: Indians never attack caravans.

7 p.m.: Dinner is served! Unfortunately, tonight, like every night, you have to eat dry bread and bacon.

9 p.m.: Beddy-bye-time! You have really deserved a good rest! You don't even mind sleeping on the ground because you are so exhausted that you fall asleep in a second!

THE SETTLER'S TEST

Are the following statements true or false? Check your answers on the answers page, add up your score and see if you would have been able to live as a pioneer.

- It was often very windy on the Great Prairies. Based on this observation, a rather entrepreneurial inventor put together a Pioneer's Sailing Wagon. The prototype seemed to work for a few rather exciting yards, after which the driver lost control and the wagon crashed and were destroyed.

TRUE   **FALSE**

- Once again, on the subject of strange methods of transport: dozens of pioneers left for the conquest of the West with men pushing wheel barrows instead of oxen pulling wagons. What an effort!

TRUE   **FALSE**

- One of the most difficult things to find in the middle of the prairies was wood to burn, whereas buffalo dung was plentiful. What do you use to cook the dinner? The pioneers burned the buffalo dung as fuel for the camp fire.

TRUE   **FALSE**

- Because there was much buffalo dung to be found along the Oregon Trail, the children began to use it to play with, throwing them like Frisbees!

TRUE   **FALSE**

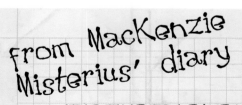

From MacKenzie Misterius' diary

IT IS TIME TO LEAVE MY SETTLER FRIENDS AND FOLLOW THE CLUES TO SOLVE THE INDIAN MYSTERY OF MIC-KO-SUC. TO FIND OUT MY NEXT DESTINATION, READ THE LETTERS BY FOLLOWING THE ARROWS.

T E R A P A R E
H G E T R I I S

GREAT PRAIRIES

"Alex!" protested Penny, after the umpteenth jerk of the hot-air balloon that had made her fly to the other side of Epsilon.

"Sorry Penny, but it is really difficult to stay on course without any landmarks, like a tree or a mountain. We are flying over a sea of grass!"

"Now do you understand why they are called the 'great' prairies? Ouch! Alex!" Penny got up from the floor of the basket, where she had fallen after Epsilon's most recent sudden swerve.

"Ehm... sorry little sister... I need to set a course." Alex leaned out of the hot-air balloon observing the boundless plains that extended below them, first with an expression of admiration but gradually becoming more distressed. After several minutes of observation, however, he turned to Penny with an expression of satisfaction and pointed out to her something he had caught sight of in the distance. "Look little sister! I shall use that little brown mark as a landmark," he said, pointing to a little spot that stuck out on the green prairie. Penny looked with the telescope in the direction pointed out by her brother.

"Alex... your landmark is moving! Alex... it's galloping towards us! Alex... It's a group of animals, thousands of them!"

"Wow! They're bison! It's an enormous herd of bison!" shouted Alex, jumping and gesticulating in the direction of the moving herd. "Penny, get MacKenzie Misterius' diary. I remember that there was something on bison and other prairie animals."

22

DID YOU KNOW?
It is estimated that, at the beginning of the 19th century, it was possible to catch sight of herds of thousands of bison in the prairies and that in the whole North American territory there were about 70 million bison. Unfortunately, the conquest of the West marked the beginning of ruthless hunting of bison, sought after for their meat and fur. Over a few decades these animals were decimated and today only a few hundred survive.

Mother bison helps her little one, with a mighty lick, to get up for the first time.

WHO LIVES ON THE GREAT PRAIRIES?

Do you want to discover which animals live on these immense expanses of grass? Find out by scaling the prairie food pyramid.

A FOOD PYRAMID...

… is a diagram that shows the relationships between the animals that live in the same ecosystem.
All the prairie animals depend on grass. This is the food for herbivores that, in turn, fall prey to large and small carnivores. Read the description of each animal and find the clue to place each one in the correct section of the food pyramid. If you think you have figured out its place, then write its number at the point on the pyramid that you think is correct. When you have finished, if you have put all the animals in the right places, you will always get a total of 20 by adding up the numbers on each side of the pyramid.

24

3

5

THE GREEN RATTLESNAKE

is a highly poisonous snake, characterized by the rattle at the end of its tail that it moves to frighten off enemies. A bite from this SMALL PREDATOR is lethal for its prey.

THE BISON

is the king of the prairie. It is 4 to 6 ft (1 to 2 m) in height and 8 to 13 ft (2.5 to 4 m) in length, making it the biggest terrestrial mammal of the Americas. Bison are HERBIVOROUS animals that live in herds.

8

THE GOLDEN EAGLE

has a wingspan of about 72 to 87 inches (1.8 to 2 m). To picture this, imagine an eagle with open wings that span the length of an average car. This splendid PREDATOR bird is the largest bird of prey of the prairies.

THE PRAIRIE DOG

is a small HERBIVOROUS RODENT, about 12 to 15 inches (30 to 40 cm) long, and is one of the symbols of the North American prairie because it is very widespread. It is called a 'dog' because when it makes its characteristic noise, it sounds like barking.

9

10

THE WOLF

is a LARGE PREDATOR that can also be found in other habitats that are quite different from the prairies, such as the forests of the Rocky Mountains. Wolves usually hunt in packs.

7

THE PRONGHORN

is a HERBIVORE that resembles both antelopes and goats mainly because of its agility and the speed it can reach when running: about 40 mph (64 kph). The pronghorn uses its speed to flee predators.

6

THE BADGER

with its little sleepy face and the white stripe on its head is quite unmistakable. It does not look like an aggressive animal but, in fact, the badger is one of the SMALL PREDATORS of the prairie. It is a carnivore that hunts mainly rodents and reptiles.

FOOD PYRAMID

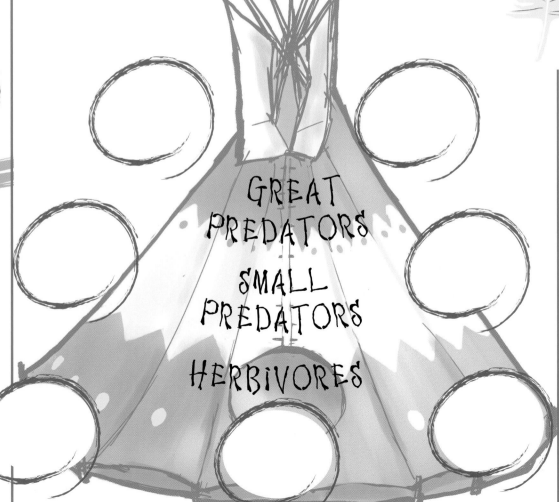

GREAT PREDATORS

SMALL PREDATORS

HERBIVORES

Alex and Penny looked at the watch in amazement. The bison were so numerous that the galloping herd had taken more than three hours to pass under the hot-air balloon! It was such a fascinating spectacle that the twins had not been able to take their eyes off it for a minute, but now Penny looked around her and noticed that the sun was setting.

"Alex, it's getting dark, what are we going to do?"

"My goodness, how late it is! We'll have to find something to eat, I'm really hungry!"

"Well, if you come down from that flying contraption I'll give you some beans," said an unfamiliar voice. The twins leaned out of the hot-air balloon and saw a camp fire right under Epsilon, and a boy who was more or less their age and who, because of his shapeless clothes and old hat, looked just like...

"A cowboy!! Are you a real cowboy?" a hopeful Alex asked him.

"Well friend, as far as I know... yes! My name is Johnny Spur, and I am camping here with the herd for the night." The children got down from Epsilon and walked toward the fire.

"Do you want some beans then?" Penny looked suspiciously at the black iron skillet, which did not appear to have been washed for weeks. "Thank you but..."

"Of course! I can't wait to try a real cowboy's beans!" answered Alex with enthusiasm as he sat down by the fire. "I want to know everything about your work! You know, I'd like to become a cowboy as well! What do I have to do?"

"Well, friend, for a start let me say that your clothes are really strange! You have to dress like a real cowboy first. Look at me, for example!"

JOHNNY SPUR

If you want to look like a cowboy, see how
Johnny Spur dresses.

HAT: protects from the rain and the sun. A real cowboy is never separated from his Stetson hat, thus called because it was designed by John Stetson.

BANDANA: a cotton or silk handkerchief that is tied round the neck and raised over the face to protect it from the sun and the dust raised by the hooves of the herds.

LASSO: the rope a cowboy always carries rolled up on the saddle. It is used to 'bridle' the animals thanks to a noose made at one end that the cowboy throws with great accuracy.

SPURS: the spurs are found on the heels of the boots, and the cowboy pushes them against the horse's sides to make it set off at a gallop.

LEATHER TROUSER COVERS: cowboys call them chaps. They are indispensable to protect the legs from the shrubs and cactus spines.

27

BETSY HAS ESCAPED

Betsy is the most unruly and curious little calf of the herd and she never loses a chance to wander away and get into trouble.
Help Johnny Spur to go down the only way possible to get to Betsy and, when you get to the crossroads, slow down to read something interesting about cowboys' difficult lives.

"Cowboy" is how the tireless herders were called when, between 1866 and 1888, they had the task of driving enormous herds from the south to the north of the United States.

The herds were rounded up in spring by chasing and capturing Longhorn cows that ran wild on the plains of Texas.

28

The Longhorns were the descendants of the cattle brought to America by the Spanish conquistadores at the end of the 16th century. Left free in the prairies, these animals had gone back to living wild, reproducing undisturbed and reaching, in the 19th century, a record number.

The cowboys were involved in rounding up and guiding herds of about 5000 cattle and covering at least 6 miles per day. Each cowboy was responsible for 250 animals, and had several horses in order to always be ready to chase after unruly calves like Betsy.

As you will have figured out a cowboy's life was dangerous, hard and tiring: every day these tireless herders rode for at least 12 hours, through dust, under the merciless sun of the prairies or the beating rain, eating around a fire and sleeping on the ground. The only place where they could find, for a short period, any home comfort was the RANCH!

WELCOME TO THE RANCH!

From MacKenzie Misterius' diary
28th September: I have finally arrived at the ranch! The first impression is that of a place in the middle of nowhere: the ranch is made up of several buildings, which make it almost completely independent, like a small town. I am really curious to discover everything about it.

At the heart of the ranch is the owner's or supervisor's home. The house's appearance surprised me because it's very simple. The walls, for example, are made of wooden logs with moss and mud to fill in the gaps.

The cowboys' horses stay in the stable during their brief stays at the ranch. The person who looks after the horses is called a wrangler.

Around the owner's house are various cabins, each serving a purpose. One, for example, is the cabin where meals are cooked and eaten. The supplies come from the nearest town. "Nearest" so to speak, seeing as the town is 300 miles from here.

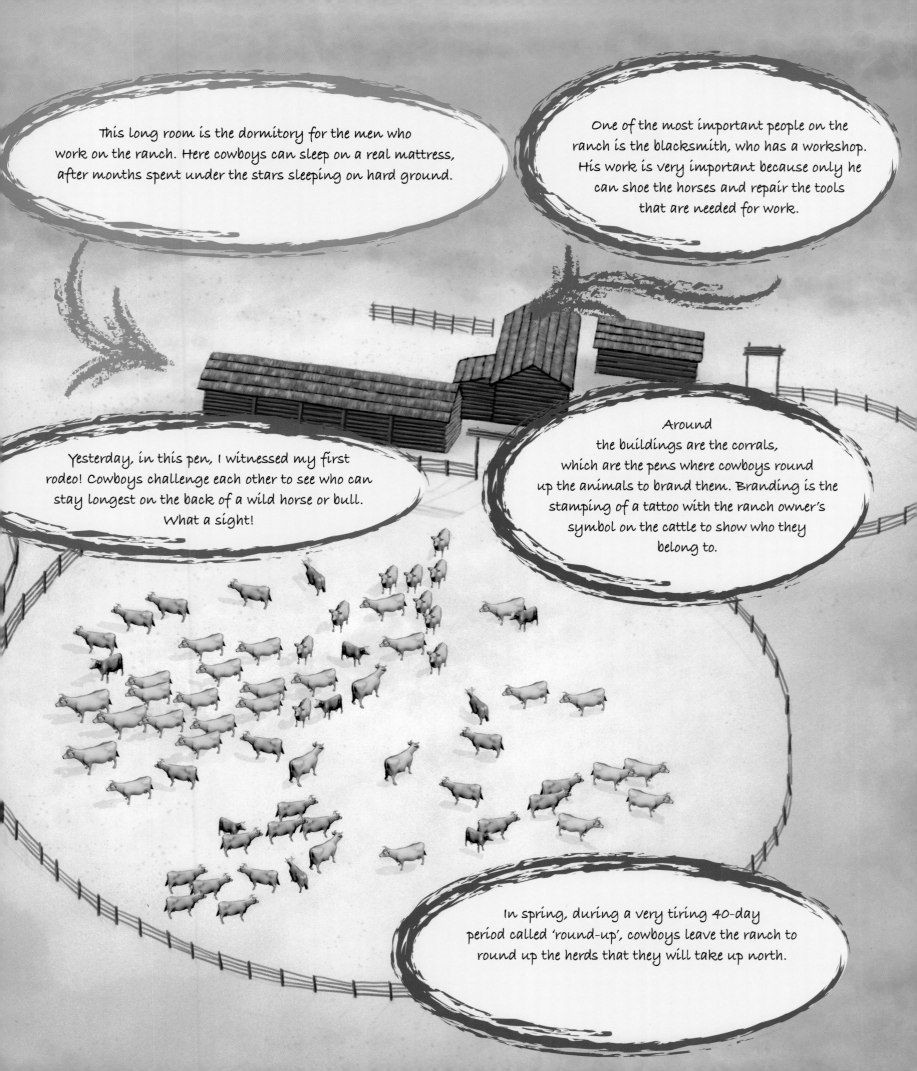

HORSES OF THE WEST

Johnny Spur looked critically at the twins as they were putting on the cowboy clothes. Alex was beside himself: he had never got dressed so quickly and with such enthusiasm! Penny, for her part, was far more worried about the smell of the jacket that she had in her hand. Goodness knows how long it was since it had last been washed! She decided, however, to pretend not to notice and made at the cowboy a little unconvincing smile, which completely disappeared as soon as she heard his next comment.

"Nothing doing: there is something missing! You will never look like real cowboys without a horse! Luckily I have one here for you! It's named Pat Hock."

"A horse!" The twins exclaimed in unison but with two completely different tones: Alex was literally going mad with joy, whereas Penny was looking at it in disbelief.

"Alex! We can't take a horse with us! We have Epsilon to move about in! Alex? Aleeex?"

"Penny, look at it!" Alex hugged the horse that Johnny had pointed out to him. Have you seen what an intelligent expression! In reality, the animal seemed rather bored, even if it was really enjoying Alex's petting!

"Don't worry, Penny, that horse knows the West like its hooves! It will be a great guide and, when you have to leave, it will be able to find the way back home. You can't do without it! Do you know how important it is to have a horse around here?"

THE STAGECOACH

From 4 to 6 horses were needed to pull a stagecoach: one of the fastest means of transport for the wealthier travelers of the time. Each carriage could carry a maximum of 18 passengers who undertook very dangerous journeys: stagecoaches were often, in fact, one of the favorite targets for gangs of bandits hanging about in the West! The journey from the Pacific to the Mississippi took 25 days by stagecoach as opposed to six months by wagon. So, if you were in a hurry it was worth taking the risk… at least until the railway was built.

THE TRAIN IS COMING...ON A SINGLE TRACK!

Between 1864 and 1869 a monumental work of construction was achieved, which for the time was a triumph and destined to radically change the life and nature of the West: the railway. The construction of the railway was completed in a record time of five years thanks to the decision to give the work to two companies that had the task of meeting each other half way coming from opposite directions: Union Pacific, which worked its way west, and Central Pacific, which worked its way east.

The historic meeting took place at Promontory Point in Utah, on 10th May, 1869. To commemorate the event the presidents of the two companies, who arrived by train, placed the last spike that, for the occasion, had been made out of solid gold.

A RECORD TRAIN!

Discover some 'record' numbers that marked the construction of the railway

The thousands of Chinese employed by Central Pacific for the construction were known as coolies.

10,000 workmen in total were employed by Union Pacific. Most of them were of Irish origin.

Approximately **20 million** spikes (nails) were used.

Approximately **4 million** wooden ties were used.

2 large mountain ranges were crossed by the tracks.

6 days were necessary to cover the distance by train between New York and San Francisco!

from MacKenzie
Misterius's diary

THE NAME OF MY NEXT DESTINATION IS HIDDEN INSIDE THE DIAGRAM BELOW: TO DECIPHER IT, BLACK OUT ALL THE OCCURRENCES OF THE LETTERS K AND Z.

KKTZKKHZZKEKK
ZCKKOKLZZKKKKK
ZZOZKRKKZKKKK
AKKDKKZOKKZRK
KIKVZZZKKKEKZRK

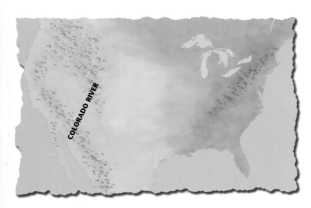

34

"Neiiiiiigh!"

"No! You move, stupid nag!"

"Penny, don't shout at my charger."

"Alex! I've got his tail in my face! Tell me why your horse has to fly in the hot-air balloon rather than following us at a gallop?"

"Epsilon is too fast for any animal! Even for Pat Hock, isn't it?"

"Neiiiiiigh!" Pat Hock agreed noisily shaking his mane and rolling his eyes.

"Well said! Little sister, stop moaning and try to take your mind off it. Why don't you read MacKenzie's diary to us?"

"All right, even if it is difficult to read with a tail in front of my eyes... his is what MacKenzie writes: 'I am coming to the Colorado River to check whether the rumors I have heard are true. It would appear that gold has been found even here! If this is the case, what happened in the place where it started 10 years ago could repeat itself, the so-called Gold Rush, California. This region was, until 1848, unknown to most Americans, and San Francisco was only a little port inhabited by a few hundred people. Within a few years thousands of people arrived, drawn by the dream of finding gold and becoming rich in a short time. To tell the truth...'"

"Gold!" Alex interrupted the diary reading and increased the speed of the hot-air balloon. Quick, we must get there before the others!"

"Alex, you don't want to start looking for gold, do yo?"

"But of course! A new video game has come out... I have to find a nice nugget, so that when we go home I can buy it!"

"Alex, don't be silly! Do you think it is easy to find gold?"

"Of course! That is the Colorado down there. Let's land and start looking for a nice big nugget straight away."

"What do you say Pat?"

"Neiiiiiiiiiiiiigh!"

"How naïve! Looking for gold is certainly not that easy and the gold prospectors didn't have an easy time of it. Listen to what MacKenzie Misterius had to say about it."

The Colorado River has its source in the Rocky Mountains and flows, for 1600 miles, along a desert plateau in which it has hollowed out long deep canyons.

In the 18th century, Francisco Tomas Garcés, a Spanish missionary who was an explorer at heart, reached the river's banks and, observing its reddish waters, decided to baptize it 'Colorado' – meaning "colored river."

DID YOU KNOW?

The Gold Rush started in 1849, and for this reason the gold prospectors were also called the '49ers.' They weren't all American: gold fever also infected Mexicans, Chinese, Germans, French and many others, who came in from all over the world. The prospectors invaded California and, from 1859 on, they also moved onto the banks of the Colorado River.

GOLD FEVER BECOMES AN EPIDEMIC!

If you actually found a gold deposit in your garden, what would you do? Perhaps you would jump for joy or perhaps you would dash to tell all your friends to make them mad with jealousy. In reality, the man who first found gold in California reacted very differently – he lost hope and tried to hide it for as long as possible. Do you want to know why? Read his story.

JOHN SUTTER was one of the most well-known men in California. He had reached this part of the world in 1839 with the intention of creating an agricultural empire. Ten years later his dream seemed to have come true, but there was a surprise in store. In 1847, he gave James Marshall the task of building a barn on the banks of the American River.

The work was almost finished when Marshall noticed a strange flash in the waters of the river.

It was **January 24th, 1848** when Marshall found the first gold nugget.

Both men realized that this find would attract thousands of people to the area and they decided to protect Sutter's land from such an invasion. However, news of the find spread anyway and there were those who thought of taking advantage of it. A San Francisco merchant, **Sam Brannan**, understood that the arrival of the gold prospectors could make him rich and so he spread the news about finding gold, which marked the beginning of the gold fever that attracted more than 100,000 people to California, making him indeed one of the richest men in the country. How? Here is an example: a shovel that had been selling in his shops for 20 cents, was worth 15 dollars after the announcement! Sutter's destiny was very different because, as he had foreseen, his land was invaded by seekers and his empire fell to pieces. One of the richest men in California became poor because of finding gold!

MINER'S MAZE

Are you ready to work for hours, up to your knees in the freezing water of the river sieving tons of earth in the hope of seeing a flash of gold among the sand? Would you be able to cope with the disappointment of working for days, and sometimes months, without getting any results? If your answer is yes, start working! Try to find your first gold nugget by finding the only path that allows you to pick up all the tools for the job: the pan, the cradle and the long-tom..

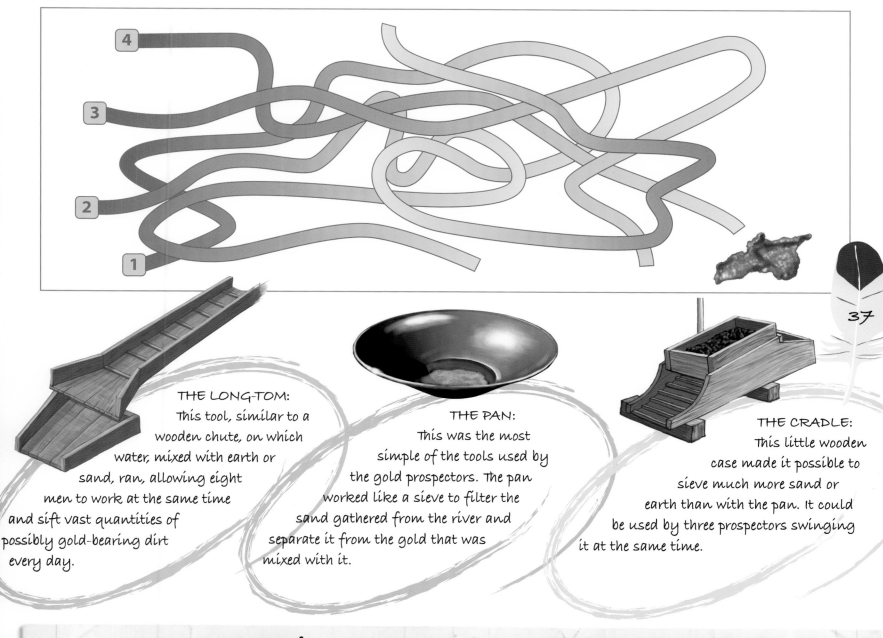

THE LONG-TOM:
This tool, similar to a wooden chute, on which water, mixed with earth or sand, ran, allowing eight men to work at the same time and sift vast quantities of possibly gold-bearing dirt every day.

THE PAN:
This was the most simple of the tools used by the gold prospectors. The pan worked like a sieve to filter the sand gathered from the river and separate it from the gold that was mixed with it.

THE CRADLE:
This little wooden case made it possible to sieve much more sand or earth than with the pan. It could be used by three prospectors swinging it at the same time.

MacKenzie Misterius' diary says

IT IS TIME TO SAY GOODBYE TO YOUR MINER FRIENDS AND GO BACK ONTO THE TRACES OF THE INDIAN MYSTERY CALLED MIC-KO-SUC. DO YOU WANT TO KNOW WHERE I INTEND TO GO? BLACK OUT THE SPACES WITH THE NUGGETS AND YOU WILL FIND OUT.

GRAND CANYON

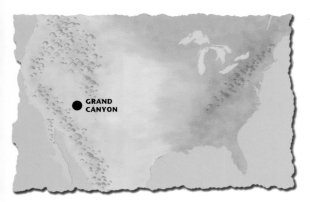

GRAND CANYON

38

"Come on Alex, stop sulking! Did you really think that it would have been so easy for us to find a gold nugget?"
"Yes! Johnny Spur told me that Pat Hock was a gold prospector for a while, weren't you Pat?"
"Neiiiiiiiigh!"
"If anything it was a gold prospector's horse and a horse is not like a truffle dog: it can't smell gold. Penny looked at her travel companions who were absolutely devastated by the fruitless search, sighed and shook her head."

"Now that's enough of those long faces! Do you know where we are going? We are going to fly over one of the most famous natural wonders of the world: the Grand Canyon!" Alex seemed to cheer up when he heard these words.
"I know the Grand Canyon! It is one of the settings of my video game! It is a chasm formed by the Colorado River, isn't it Penny?"
"Right, little brother! A chasm that's 5250 ft (1600 m) deep and 275 miles (442 km) long. An extraordinary and impressive sight!"
"It is one of the most visited places in the world: I think that I read on the internet that every year the Grand Canyon attracts more than 5 million tourists."
"This is the situation today, but during his visit MacKenzie noted in his diary the statement of an army official who was making a map of the area. Listen to what he said: 'Ours is certainly the first and, without doubt, also the last group of white people to visit these places, from which there is no gain to be had'."
"Erm…I have the feeling that his predictions were not quite right! Were they Pat?"
"Neiiiiiiiiiiigh!"

DID YOU KNOW?
The first man who succeeded navigating the rivers through the Grand Canyon was the explorer and geologist John Wesley Powell. After 98 days of navigation in the dangerous waters of the Colorado River, the exploit was accomplished on 29th August, 1869.

The Grand Canyon is considered to be one of the wonders of the world.

The Grand Canyon Territory was declared a national monument in 1908 and a national park in 1919.

The Grand Canyon was formed by the Colorado River, which hollowed it out at the speed of barely an inch per century!

A STAGGERING SIGHT!

Standing on the edge of the Grand Canyon and staring into the chasm that drops away beneath you means looking at 2 billion years of the history of our planet! The canyon opened by the Colorado River has in fact exposed various strata of rock to the surface. Each strata layer traced by geologists reveals ever more distant periods the further down the canyon they study.

40

There are as many as 12 different rock formations.

At the top of all the other layers is a formation made up of grey limestone called Kaibab, rich in sea fossils that date back to the time when the sea covered this area. Even though it is the 'youngest' layer, it already existed at the time of the dinosaurs!

The layers have different colors according to the minerals contained in the rocks. The reddish colour of the canyon walls is mainly due to large quantities of iron present in many of the layers.

The oldest layer is to be found at the bottom of the canyon: it is made up of a stone called Vishnu shale. How old is it? About 2000 million years!

BECOME AN APPRENTICE RANGER!

Would you like to be a Grand Canyon ranger? Would you like to be a guardian of Nature and accompany visitors to discover the secrets of the Canyon?

Answer the quiz questions and check your knowledge of the Grand Canyon using the information from the previous pages. There is a color for every correct answer: use it to color the spaces of the diagram that correspond to the number of the question. When the game is over you will find out what is hiding between the rocks of the canyon.

1 - HOW MANY ROCK FORMATIONS ARE VISIBLE?

■ 8

■ 10

■ 12

2 - WHAT IS VISHNU?

■ The oldest layer of the Grand Canyon

■ The most recent layer of the Grand Canyon

■ A Hindu sanctuary built on the bottom of the canyon

3 - WHAT IS KAIBAB?

■ The oldest layer of the Grand Canyon

■ The most recent layer of the Grand Canyon

■ A sandwich that is sold at the stall near the car park

4 - WHICH MINERAL MAKES THE ROCKS RED?

■ Magnesium

■ Iron

■ Limestone

5 - HOW OLD IS THE VISHNU LAYER?

■ 2 million years

■ 200 million years

■ 2000 million years

6 - AT WHAT SPEED DID THE COLORADO RIVER HOLLOW OUT THE ROCK OF THE CANYON?

■ Less than 1 inch per hour

■ Less than 1 inch per year

■ Less than 1 inch per century

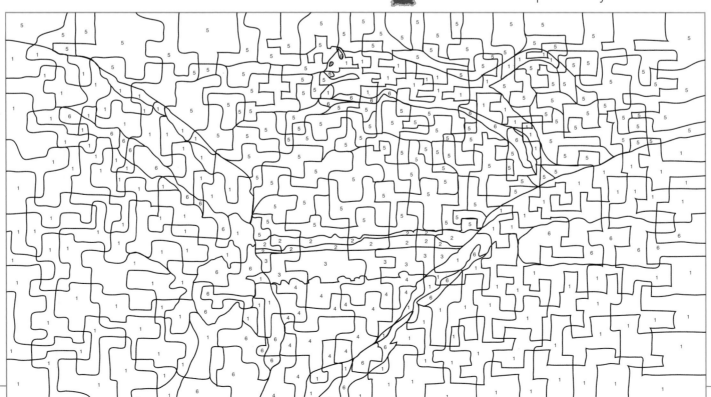

NATURE IN THE GRAND CANYON

Even if at first sight the Grand Canyon can give the impression of being a desert zone, in reality its gorges are inhabited by a very rich and varied fauna made up of as many as 75 different species of mammals, 50 species of reptiles and amphibians, 25 species of fish and 300 species of birds. Out of all these animals, two have been chosen to face each other in a very special challenge: the puma and the coyote. Both are inhabitants of the Grand Canyon and will compete to find out who will reach the finish line first! You will become the impartial referee of the competition between the puma and the coyote. Only you, indeed, can make these two animals go forward along the course of the competition. Here are the rules of the game: read the characteristics of the puma and the coyote and try to understand which of the two is the largest, the fastest, the smartest and so on. The winner of the competition will be able to go forward on the path for as many spaces as the question suggests. When you have answered all the questions you will find out which animal will come in first.

1 WHICH IS HIGHEST?
(this question is worth 3 squares)
- The puma's back is 26 to 32 inches (66 to 80 cm) high
- The coyote's back is 23 to 26 inches (58 to 66 cm) high

3 WHICH IS THE NOISIEST?
(this question is worth 5 squares)
- The puma is a solitary animal and so usually it has nobody to 'talk' to but, on certain occasions, it can roar or purr.
- The Latin name for the coyote is Canis latrans, meaning 'barking dog.' The coyote deserves this name because it is able to bark in as many as 11 different ways, which are so noisy that they can be heard up to 2.5 miles away!

2 WHICH IS THE LONGEST?
(this question is worth 5 squares)
- The coyote is about 4 ft (1.25 m) long
- The puma is 5 to 9 ft (1.5 to 2.5 m) long

4 WHICH IS THE LIGHTEST?
(this question is worth 6 squares)
- The puma weighs 70 to 190 lb (32 to 86 kg)
- The coyote weighs 18 to 44 lb (8 to 20 kg)

5 WHICH IS THE SMARTEST?
(this question is worth 7 squares)
- The coyote has worked out a plan for hunting. It behaves as if it were mad, jumping and whining, in front of a group of birds while one of his friends creeps in and leaps on the distracted birds.
- The puma's technique is just as efficient but less imaginative. It leaps on its prey and breaks its neck bone with a powerful bite.

6 WHICH IS THE MOST DANGEROUS TO HUMANS?
(this question is worth 4 squares)
- The puma does not usually attack people but occasionally this can happen, especially if it encounters people traveling at night, dawn or in fog – probably, in such cases, it mistakes them for prey.
- The coyote is very curious but he never goes anywhere near people but instead just watches them from a distance.

7 WHICH IS THE LESS PROLIFIC
(this question is worth 3 squares)
- The puma becomes the proud parent of 2 or 3 kittens once a year
- The coyote, becomes the proud parent of 5 to 7 pups in spring.

8 WHICH IS THE LESS PICKY?
(this question is worth 3 squares)
- The coyote is a very widespread animal because it is very good at adapting to the place in which it lives. Indeed, it can feed on mice, rabbits, insects, fish, snakes, fruit, frogs and, if it is in a town, even cats and rubbish!
- 90% of the puma's diet is made up of venison. A puma would never eat either carrion or reptiles.

MacKenzie Misterius' diary says:

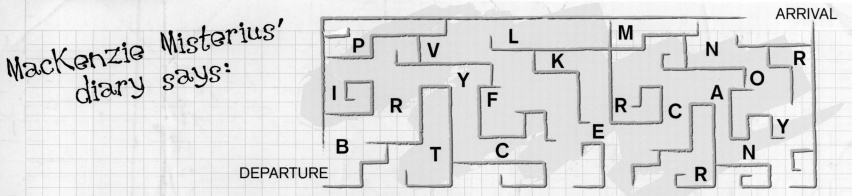

DEPARTURE

ARRIVAL

IT IS A SHAME TO LEAVE BEHIND SUCH A MAJESTIC PLACE BUT MY JOURNEY MUST GO ON! WHAT WILL BE MY NEXT DESTINATION? TO FIND OUT HOW TO GO THROUGH THE MAZE, READ AS YOU GO ON THE LETTERS THAT YOU MEET ON YOUR WAY!

DID YOU KNOW?

"A cursed place to lose a cow." It was with these words that Colonel Ebenezer Bryce defined the canyon where he had lived with his wife Mary, trying to make an ill-fated attempt at cattle breeding flourish. Tired of losing his cows among the stone spires, Ebenezer decided to move away after just five years. Although he left, his name remains – this <u>area</u> in southern Utah has been known since that time as Bryce Canyon.

As she was checking the course on the computer on-board Epsilon, every now and then Penny glanced at her brother engrossed in reading Misterius' great-great-great-uncle's diary.

"Alex, could you have a look at the screen? We should have already arrived at Bryce Canyon."

"Just wait a second, little sister, I have to finish reading the page."

"Alex, I'm really proud of you! You are finally getting interested in something more exciting than your video game!"

"Very exciting! Reading MacKenzie's diary I have found a lot of information about life in the West! For example, did you know that the settlers used a cream obtained by mixing ashes and boiling water instead of soap? It was called lye. And do you know that there is a thorny plant that grows on the prairies that is succulent and nutritious? It is the prickly pear. All these strange things will certainly be useful to help me to go on to the next stage of the game where I've been stuck for weeks!"

"I thought it was strange! Alex, we have arrived at the Bryce Canyon National Park. What do you say about reading some information that will help us to go on to the next stage?"

"Ok! As far as I can understand, MacKenzie came to the Canyon to visit the Indian chief of the Paiute tribe to ask for his help in solving the Mic-Ko-Suc Indian mystery. Listen to what he wrote: 'Spires and rocks all around! A continuous succession of red stone buttes! This canyon can only be crossed by somebody who possesses a pair of wings!'"

"Or a hot-air balloon!" added Penny, chuckling.

"I think it will be difficult even with Epsilon, little sister. Look underneath us: it looks like a stone maze! There are hundreds of spires hollowed out in the rock! According to MacKenzie's diary, they are called 'hoodoos.' All these spires have been formed by the erosion of the Paunsaugunt plateau, which, in the Paiute Indian language means 'home of the beaver.' Well, it must have been an enormous beaver to gnaw the rocks like that!"

45

The rock erosion proceeds in record time, from a geological point of view – as much as 1 inch (2.5 cm) every 65 years!

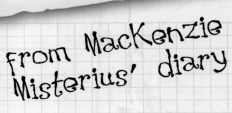

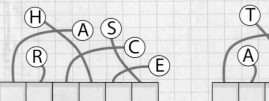
from MacKenzie Misterius' diary

UNFORTUNATELY, THE PAIUTE INDIANS WERE NOT ABLE TO HELP ME BUT THEY SUGGESTED THAT I VISIT A PLACE NEARBY WHERE RUPESTRIAN (CAVE OR ROCK) INSCRIPTIONS BY THE ANCIENT ANASAZI INDIAN POPULATION CAN BE SEEN. TO FIND OUT WHAT MY NEXT DESTINATION IS, REPLACE THE SYMBOLS WITH LETTERS.

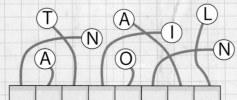

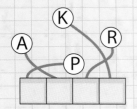

As well as the puma, there are about 200 animal species in the park, including birds, gray wolves, coyotes and lizards.

DID YOU KNOW?
Some arches have funny or strange names such as, for example, the rocks called the 'Three Gossips' or 'Eye of the Whale.' The elegant 'Delicate Arch' is the most famous of the formations in the park, so much so that it has become a symbol of the state of Utah.

ARCHES NATIONAL PARK

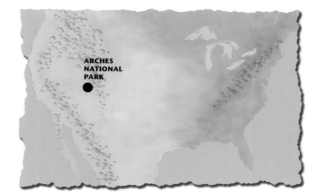

"Alex, listen to what MacKenzie Misterius wrote in his diary: 'September 13th. I decided to visit this desert zone characterized by formations that resemble stone bridges, because I was told that, on these rocks, there are engravings left hundreds of years ago by Indian populations. I hope to find information that will help me solve the Mic-Ko-Suc mystery.' It would appear that we shall know that we are in the right place when we catch sight of the strange rock formations."

"Lift your head up from that diary, little sister, and look out of the hot-air balloon. If I am not mistaken, that is a strange rock formation," said Alex pointing out an elegant red stone arch that rose a few feet below them.

"WOW!!" exclaimed Penny amazed. "It would appear that we have arrived! We are flying over the Arches National Park."

"I think so. The natural park is famous for the natural arches. I am starting the maneuver for landing. I can't wait to try and climb some of those arches! I want to go underneath them, try to sit astride one of them and see if I can. . . ."

"Neiiiiiiiiiiiiiigh!" All of a sudden Pat Hock started to kick and shake his mane irritably throwing Penny to the opposite side of the hot-air balloon.

"Alex, could you tell your nag not to kick?"

"What's the matter Pat? Keep calm. I have never seen him so restless! Maybe he wants to go down. Don't worry Pat we're landing straight away."

On hearing these words Pat Hock did not calm down at all but reared up on his two hind legs and rolled his eyes snorting.

"W…w…wait Alex!" stammered Penny. "Don't land! Look down there, at the bottom of the arch: there is a puma!"

"AAARGH! I hadn't seen it! We were about to land next to a puma! That's why Pat was agitated!! Well done Pat!" screamed Alex, throwing his arms round the horse's neck. Penny followed suit: this time she could not criticize Pat Hock's behavior at all!

In the Arches National Park there is the highest concentration of stone arches to be found in the world: there are about 2000.

47

from MacKenzie Misterius' diary

THE ENGRAVINGS ON THE ROCKS WERE CARVED BY THE ANASAZI INDIANS HUNDREDS OF CENTURIES AGO: I WANT TO TRY AND FOLLOW THIS TRAIL! MY NEXT DESTINATION WILL BE AN ANASAZI INDIAN VILLAGE. TO FIND OUT WHAT THE VILLAGE IS CALLED, CHANGE THE ORDER OF THE LETTERS BELOW.

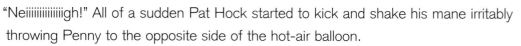

⊹ = A	❋ = D	⊹ = G	✳ = O	◗ = T
ⵝ = B	↯ = E	❂ = I	✦ = R	✛ = U
✛ = C	↡ = F	❉ = M	◈ = S	ⵗ = V

The word Anasazi derives from a Navajo term meaning "the ancients." The Anasazi culture, as the remains of villages in stone such as that of Mesa Verde testify, was founded in about AD 900 and ceased to exist about 700 years later.

DID YOU KNOW?
That the native populations of the American continent were called 'Indians' like the inhabitants of India due to an error! When Christopher Columbus landed, in 1492, on the American coast, he was certain that he had reached India and thought he was right in calling the inhabitants "Indians." What a mistake!

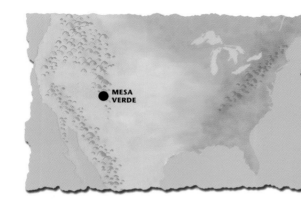

"We have arrived, little sister. We shall land right there on those rocks heaped one on top of the other."

"No Alex! Those are not just any old rocks! They are the remains of a house from the city of Mesa Verde!"

"City? Well! I can't see any city."

"Penny glanced at Alex in exasperation: "You haven't listened to one word that I have said!" Alex looked at her with a guilty expression. "It's not true! Maybe I missed the odd detail, but only because I was busy flying Epsilon! Why don't you refresh my memory with the most important details. In the meantime, get down from the hot-air balloon, Princess. We have landed where you wished." Pat Hock jumped out of the hot-air balloon with great agility and started to graze, with great satisfaction, on an enormous clump of grass. Penny, on the other hand, sat down under a boulder and started to tell the whole thing from the beginning. "What we can see inside the cave are the remains of Mesa Verde, a large city built in the 15th century by an Indian tribe called the Anasazi."

"And where are all these Sasalazi now?"

"Anasazi, not Sasalazi, and what happened to them is still a mystery!" declared the happy voice of a boy behind them.

The children turned in amazement towards the new arrival, exclaiming in chorus: "Who are you?" But the stranger didn't have time to answer. Alex observed his clothes made from soft deerskin, decorated with drawings and beads. He also noticed the bow that the boy was carrying nonchalantly on his back and the small feather that stuck out above his head.

"You're an Indian!" screamed Alex at last.

"Indian? Well, I suppose that's how you pale faces would call us Native Americans."

"Alex didn't mean to offend you. Believe me. What is your name?"

"My name is Crooked Moon."

"Wow! You are the first Indian I have ever met! Which tribe do you belong to? Are you a Sioux? A Fox? An Iowa?"

"I belong to the Navajo tribe. Even if we call ourselves Dine, which, in my language means 'people'."

"Ah, it doesn't matter, anyway it's the same thing."

"What did you say? I have never been so insulted in my life!" Crooked Moon straightened the long knife that he carried in his belt, took his bow in his right hand and . . .

"What…what do you want to do?"stammered Alex. "I'm sorry if I offended you but don't shoot an arrow at me, don't remove my scalp!"

"Why should I?" asked Crooked Moon in amazement. "I was only making myself comfortable. You have spoken with the voice of ignorance, and therefore it is only right that I forgive you and explain to you what you don't know."

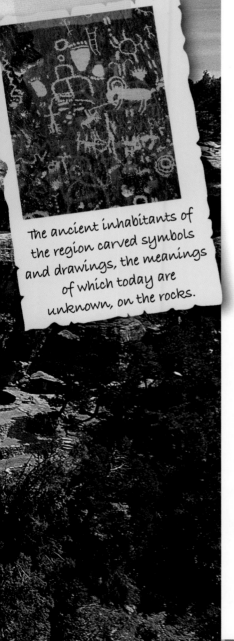

The ancient inhabitants of the region carved symbols and drawings, the meanings of which today are unknown, on the rocks.

49

THE "INDIAN NATIONS"

Before the conquest of the West, immense territories between the Mississippi River and the Pacific Ocean were inhabited only by the People of the Prairie, or, as you pale faces would say, by the American Indians. Even I don't know how many Indian nations exist but certainly there are hundreds, each with its own language, history and traditions. The most well-known tribes are the Apache, the Cheyenne, the Sioux and the Navajo. You can see where these tribes live by looking at the map.

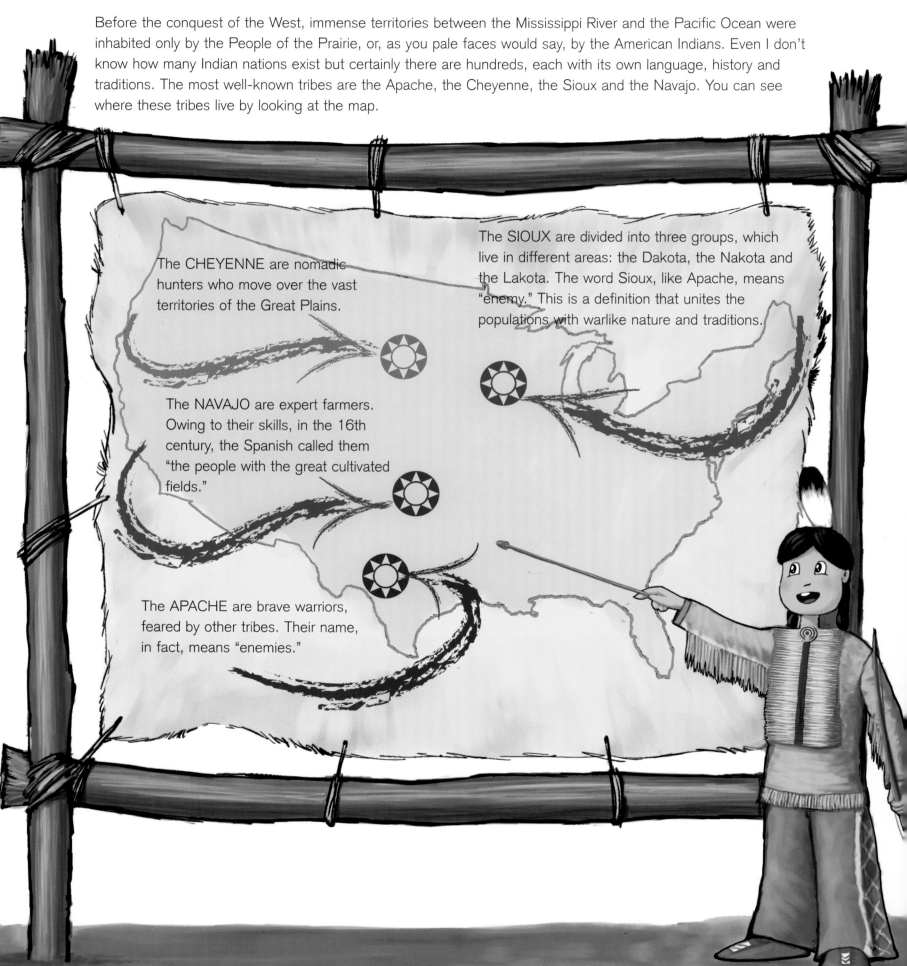

The CHEYENNE are nomadic hunters who move over the vast territories of the Great Plains.

The SIOUX are divided into three groups, which live in different areas: the Dakota, the Nakota and the Lakota. The word Sioux, like Apache, means "enemy." This is a definition that unites the populations with warlike nature and traditions.

The NAVAJO are expert farmers. Owing to their skills, in the 16th century, the Spanish called them "the people with the great cultivated fields."

The APACHE are brave warriors, feared by other tribes. Their name, in fact, means "enemies."

To get a better understanding of the huge differences that exist between the tribes, try and compare the pictures of these Indian chiefs and warriors. You will notice many differences in dress, in headdress and in weapons.

51

Even the style of their homes were different. The various tribes decided to live inside or outside according to the nature of their territory and their own traditions.

The wigwam, a cabin made from branches and bark, built by the inhabitants of the northern forests.

The igloo, the choice of the populations of the far north, made from blocks of ice and snow.

The hogan, the cabin used by the Navajo, made of wood and mud with the door facing east to see the sun rising.

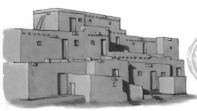

The pueblo, villages made up of small clay houses.

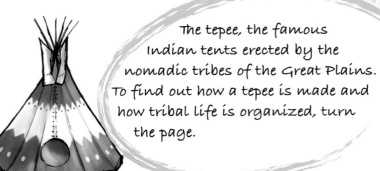

The tepee, the famous Indian tents erected by the nomadic tribes of the Great Plains. To find out how a tepee is made and how tribal life is organized, turn the page.

A HOUSE THAT IS EASY TO MOVE!

The tepee is a cone-shaped tent made of canes and bison skins, which is easy to take down and move. These are the principal requirements of the nomadic people of the Great Plains who live by hunting and who therefore must be able to move their village to follow the movements of the great bison herds.

The word tepee derives from a Lakota term which means "house."

The opening at the top allowed fires to burn inside the tent as the smoke is able to escape.

Taking down and putting up the tepee was entrusted to the women. The tepee was literally folded and loaded, for transportation, onto sleds called travois, made with the tent poles and pulled by horses.

The bison skins used to make a tepee were smoked to make them waterproof and painted with figures and symbols that represented the tribe and protected the inhabitants from evil spirits.

Inside the tepee are beds for the various family members, as well as other possessions and food.

IN A CAMP ALL THE TEPEES HAVE THEIR OPENINGS FACING EAST

The women are very busy. Among their tasks are some very tiring jobs, such as cutting and tanning the bison skins.

It is also necessary to cure the meat so that it lasts longer. To ensure this, it has to be smoked, dried and mixed with berries and fat, creating a nutritious Indian food called pemmican.

The younger male children can play round the camp and are watched by the older ones who, in the meantime, learn to hunt, ride and use a bow and arrow. The little girls, on the other hand, learn to sew and make vases and baskets as they play.

from MacKenzie Misterius' diary

HELP US TO DISCOVER THE NAME OF THE NEXT DESTINATION; WE HAVE TO PUT TOGETHER AGAIN THE PAGE FROM MACKENZIE'S DIARY, PUTTING BACK THE FRAGMENTS OF PAPER INTO THE RIGHT ORDER.

NU   EY   ME   LL   NT   VA   MO

54

The Monument Valley desert plateau was hollowed out in very ancient times by the waters of a river.

The red stone spires that interrupt the plain are called buttes or mesas, which means 'tables' in Spanish, in reference to the flat tops that characterize them.

"It was kind of you to come with us, Crooked Moon," said Penny, turning to the young Indian as she got off Pat Hock's back.

"It has been a pleasure being your guide, Penny, and to chat with you. You know many things about my people!"

"Oh, thank you, but I would like to get to know you better," answered Penny, going a little red. Alex noticed it immediately and couldn't resist the temptation to make fun of her. "Oh, yes, Crooked Moon, my sister would really like to get to know you better, wouldn't she Pat?"

"Neigh, Neiiiigh, Neiiiiiiiigh!"

"Alex! You really are stupid! I meant that I would like to visit his village and perhaps get to know something about Indian customs, that's all!" answered Penny crossly, going very red.

"You know Penny, this is a wish that can easily come true. We have almost reached my village – it's down there, look."

"WOW!" exclaimed Penny. "The countryside is beautiful!"

"Wait a moment, but I know this place. I've seen it in many westerns and it is even the setting for my video game. We are in Monument Valley!"

"I don't know what a western is or a video game, but I am happy that you like my home! Penny, you wanted to get to know my people, didn't you?"

"Yes!"

"Here we are! We are surrounded by my friends!" said Crooked Moon smiling.

Alex and Penny looked around in amazement: Crooked Moon was without doubt the only Indian they could see.

"Look again!" suggested Crooked Moon to them, chuckling.

WATCH OUT FOR THE FEATHER!

The Indians' ability to advance silently is legendary and even Crooked Moon's friends are no exception. They had slowly surrounded Alex and Penny, blending in with the surroundings in Monument Valley. Try to count how many Indians are hiding in the photograph and check that you have found them all by reading the solution on page 79.

WE ARE ALL BROTHERS

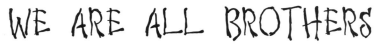

"When the earth was created with all the living beings, the Creator's intention was not only to make it livable for men.

We were put into the world with our brothers and sisters, those who have four paws, those who fly and those who swim.

All these forms of life, even the finest blade of grass and the biggest trees, form one big family with us.

We are all brothers and all equally important on this earth."

With these words, the chief of the Iroquois tribe explained the special relationship of respect that exists between Indians and Nature.

The animals, are regarded as younger brothers of men, and are the main characters in tales that the Indians use to interpret and explain their customs and physical conditions. Imagine sitting down round a fire and listening to one of these legends. Would you like to find out, for example...

WHY DO DOGS SNIFF EACH OTHER UNDER THE TAIL?

One day, a long time ago, the dogs met to elect their chief. "I propose the Bulldog as a candidate," said one of the youngest dogs. "He is a very good fighter!" "He can certainly fight but he has short legs," commented another. "I am voting for the greyhound who has long legs and can run faster than all the rest." The discussion lasted for a long time until a small tawny dog asked to speak by raising his paw and said: "I propose electing a dog that has a nice smell nice under his tail!" The proposal was accepted by everybody and the dogs immediately started sniffing each other under their tails. After several hours it was clear that none of those present smelled nice under its tail and could be the right candidate for such an important role. They would have to look elsewhere! For this reason as soon as two dogs meet, the first thing they do is sniff each other under the tail. They are still searching for their ideal chief!

Try now to invent an Indian story of your own that explains the characteristics of an animal. For example: why does the ladybird have spots? Why is the raven black?

BISON HUNTING!

The bison hunt is the most important moment in the life of the prairie inhabitants because these animals represent the most important source of survival for the tribe. Let's leave it to the Sioux Indian Lame Deer to explain to us what the bison is used for.

"The bison gave us everything we needed.... Our tepees were made from its hide. Its fur was our bed... its skin was our sacred drum... its meat gave us strength. Its stomach, into which we threw a burning stone, was the pot for the soup. Its horns were our spoons, its bones our knives and needles for our womenfolk."

RED-SKIN TO WHOM?

Among the most typical aspects of Indian culture are the colors and symbols that the warriors paint on their bodies: the so-called war paint.

These signs have a very precise meaning for Indians. Like a language the symbols can show what tribe a man belongs to, if he is a shaman or a warrior and how many enemies he has defeated in battle. The war colors also have the purpose of frightening off the enemy, and they worked perfectly with the first Europeans who arrived on Indian land. They were so stunned by the red-painted faces that they called the Indians "redskins."

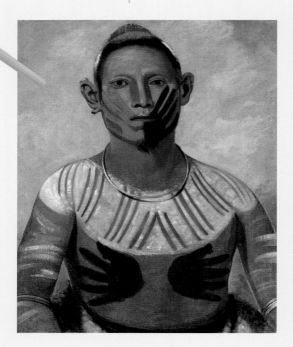

The paintings of the warrior show that he has defeated many enemies in hand-to-hand fighting.

Even the feathers worn on the head were part of a symbolic warrior language. Look at the picture of this proud warrior called "Great Darkness." The feather split into two colors of red tells us that he has been wounded many times in battle, those with the indented edge means that he has killed many enemies.

The warriors even painted the horses with symbols that identified to strangers who the horseman was. Crooked Moon painted many symbols on Pat Garretto with different meanings. The hand print means that the horseman is a warrior, the circle that he is skilled with his shield and the square that he is the leader of a group of warriors. The symbol that resembles a keyhole explains that he is about to meet a shaman.

ON THE WAR PATH

One of the greatest fears of the settlers when they were travelling on the Oregon Trail was that of meeting the Indians who were just as mysterious as they were unknown. The settlers, however, were mistaken to worry. Meetings with the tribes were nearly always peaceful and cordial. Very soon, however, things changed. The "pale faces" coming from the East Coast in ever increasing numbers started to take possession of the land on which the tribes lived and to over-hunt the game, especially the bison, the main source of survival for the Indians of the prairies. The clash between two such different cultures gave origin to a war that lasted for several years. The Indians won many battles behind some famous leaders such as Geronimo, Sitting Bull, Red Cloud and Crazy Horse, but in the end the war finished in the worst way possible for them. The tribes had to abandon the territories in which they had lived for centuries and were moved to reservations, on land that was, for the most part, poor and barren and chosen by the white people.

Geronimo, leader of the Apache tribe, was an expert warrior and respected shaman.

3500 Sioux and Cheyenne warriors united under the leadership of Sitting Bull.

61

The Indian warrior fought with various weapons:
The tomahawk was a small axe that was tied to the belt. Every tribe had a sacred tomahawk that was buried during peace time and dug up when the tribe went to war. The bow and arrows were commonly used for hunting, but they were also used for fighting. Using the bow and arrow in battle did not bring great honor on the warrior who used it because it made killing the enemy possible from a distance. The shield was made from bison skin that was treated to make it tougher and harder.

from MacKenzie Misterius' diary

TALKING TO THE CHIEF OF THE NAVAJO TRIBE HAS BEEN VERY USEFUL TO ME: HE SUGGESTED GOING TO A PLACE WHICH IS SACRED TO THE LAKOTA INDIANS, WHERE, ACCORDING TO HIM, I SHALL CERTAINLY FIND, SOMEONE WHO IS ABLE TO EXPLAIN TO ME WHAT THE MYSTERIOUS AND SACRED MIC-KO-SUC IS. THE NAME OF MY DESTINATION IS HIDDEN IN THE SMOKE SIGNALS: TO DISCOVER IT REPLACE EACH SMALL CLOUD WITH THE CORRESPONDING LETTER AND YOU WILL BE ABLE TO DECIPHER THE MESSAGE.

THE ROCKY MOUNTAINS

With a ringing whinny Pat Hock drew Penny's attention to the countryside they were flying over. "Eh! Those mountains are something else!"

"Neiiiiiiiiiiigh!"

"Ok, I admit it, this time you're right, Pat. You're not a bad guide at all! Alex, we are flying over some mountains, where are we?"

"According to the computer on board they are the peaks of the Rocky Mountains. Wait, let me ask Kappa to send me more information from headquarters."

"Are you sure we're going in the right direction?"asked Penny in a perplexed voice.

Alex looked at her frowning. That comment had wounded his pilot's pride!

"You can trust me, little sister. I am now able to guide this hot-air balloon with my eyes shut!"

"Trust you? Ah! The last time you said that, I remember…"

The BEEP of a warning light on the computer interrupted the twins before they could really start arguing.

"It's Kappa. He's sent me the information we needed. He says that the Rocky Mountains are one of the principal mountain ranges on earth, extending over the whole of North America, from Mexico to Alaska. He also says…"

"What? What else does he say, Alex?"

"Nothing."

"Alex?"

"Ok! He says that the strong winds that blow at this height have taken us slightly off course. We are heading for the Yellowstone National Park."

"Well done, pilot! Next time try not to fly with your eyes shut!"

"Ah! Keep on laughing behind my back while I ask Kappa for information on Yellowstone Park."

63

Yellowstone Park gets its name from the river which crosses it and which over the centuries has formed a canyon more than 980 ft (300 m) deep.

DID YOU KNOW?

The Rocky Mountains are made up of mountain ranges which cross the whole of North America: from the most northern point of the United States, Alaska, to the border with Mexico, in the extreme south. The highest summit of the Rocky Mountains is in Alaska: it is Mount McKinley, 20,320 ft (6194 m) high.

VISITING THE OLDEST NATIONAL PARK IN THE WORLD!

After having been inhabited for centuries by various Indian groups, the immense territory of Yellowstone, bordering on the three states of Wyoming, Montana and Idaho, was declared a national park in 1872. For the first time in history, a region unique owing to its natural characteristics was declared a protected area. Yellowstone became famous immediately for being the first national park in the world. Yellowstone Park is also famous for its 10,000 geysers.

Looking down from above it looks like the work of a brilliant painter, but, in reality the colours of this lake, which is at the heart of the park depend on the plants which live in its hot thermal waters.

The most famous geyser in the park and in the world is called Old Faithful. This name was given to it in 1870 after observing that its eruptions are regular and constant.

WHAT ARE GEYSERS?

They are very unusual hot water springs, which, at regular intervals, let out very high and spectacular columns of hot water and steam.

HOW DOES A GEYSER WORK?

The two main ingredients for having a geyser are: a water source and a great, great, deal of heat. If I were you I would not try to reproduce it in the garden or in your bath! The water collected at the source is heated by the volcanic activity under the earth's surface. The temperature becomes very high and the water starts to boil and evaporate. The steam bubbles increase the pressure at the water source until they produce an explosion that reaches the earth's surface.

A CLEVER ENGINEER

THIS CUTE RODENT CAN BUILD DAMS IN STREAMS WITH THE ACCURACY OF A SKILLED ENGINEER. DO YOU KNOW WHAT IT IS CALLED? TO FIND OUT, WRITE DOWN THE NAMES OF THE ANIMALS THAT LIVE IN THE PARK. WRITE DOWN ON THE DOTTED LINE THE LETTERS OF THE HIGHLIGHTED BOXES, IN THE RIGHT NUMERIC ORDER AND YOU WILL BE ABLE TO READ ITS NAME.

GRIZZLY
This bear can be distinguished from other bears that live in the same regions due to the hump on its back. Even though it is very aggressive and strong – it could in fact get the better of enormous animals like the bison – it is really has a soft heart and has a secret passion for honey!

BOBCAT
This cat is very similar to its European cousin, the lynx and is about double the size of a domestic cat. It is an excellent hunter and would like to eat only rabbits! It is a solitary creature that chooses a territory on which to live and defends it from intruders.

BALD EAGLE
This type of eagle, also called "white-headed," has become an absolute symbol of the United States of America. It also appears on one-dollar bills!

The DEER is one of the most numerous and timid inhabitants of the park. The males are distinguished, when adult, by long branched horns that they can use as weapons in battles.

BISON
You should already know everything about the bison! If not, go back to the Great Prairies and find out some information on this enormous but good-natured mammal.

1	2	3	V 4	5	6

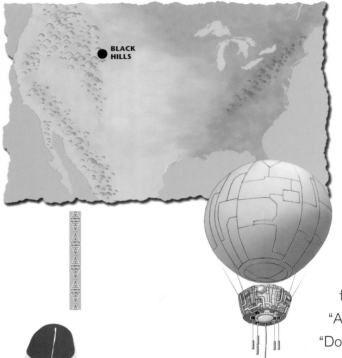

BeepBeepBeep! One of the warning lights on the computer on board Epsilon advised Alex that he had made a perfect landing! The children and Pat Hock got down from the hot-air balloon and looked at the clearing in which they had landed. "Penny, are you sure this is the right place?"

"If we have interpreted MacKenzie's directions correctly we are in the right place. These mountains are the Black Hills, sacred Indian territory, especially for the Lakota tribe. Look at these forests, Alex they are really beautiful!"

"Er... little sister... stop looking at the woods and take a look in front of us!" All of a sudden, out of the thickness of the woods appeared a tall, serious and proud looking Indian with an elaborate eagle feather headdress. He remained still and silent in front of them.

"A... Alex," stammered a frightened Penny. "What are we going to do?"

"Don't worry Penny I'll sort it out! Have you ever seen such a hat? He must be an important person. Hail, General," exclaimed Alex taking one step forward towards the Indian who stayed still and silent.

"Alex! The Indians don't have generals!"

"Er... Sir? Director? Ambassador? Little sister, what do I call him?"

"What about 'Chief'?" suggested Penny sarcastically.

"That's right! He is the chief of a tribe! Hello Chief. We are looking for this thing that is sacred to the Indians. We don't know what it is but we know that it is called Mic-Ko-Suc or something like that. Could you help us?"

"Follow me."

"Where?"

"What you are looking for is in my tent."

66

DID YOU KNOW THAT
In the Black Hills region there is Mount Rushmore, famous all over the world because on its upper flank the faces of four presidents of the United States have been sculpted: Washington, Jefferson, T. Roosevelt and Lincoln. A few miles away work is in full swing to hollow a monumental portrait of the Indian chief, Crazy Horse out of the rocky side of a hill.

The Black Hills were the scene of terrible battles between whites and Indians during the so-called "Indian Wars."

Alex and Penny looked at each other in disbelief. The Indian Chief had taken them inside his tepee where they saw an Indian who was so small that he did not reach Alex's shoulders and so old that Penny could not make out the holes where his eyes were among the thousand small wrinkles which lined his face. Notwithstanding his size, the Indian had a majestic appearance and bearing that inspired respect and fear.

The twins stared open-mouthed at the little Indian until he turned towards them and started to laugh quietly. "Eh eh eh, let me guess: you hadn't imagined that I could be a holy man, and not a sacred object."

Alex swallowed visibly. "Do you mean," he asked in a whisper, "that you are the mysterious Mic-Ko-Suc?"

"No."

The twins looked at each other completely bewildered. Who did they have in front of them? Was he or wasn't he the solution to the mystery that they had come to solve?

"Sit down and I shall explain everything, young friends. The name that you know is incomplete. This is why no Indian you have met has been able to help you: I am known as Stumickosucks! My name means, in your language, more or less 'fat from the male bison's back' definitely the best part of the meat of this sacred animal," he added, licking his lips. With this funny gesture the Indian lost most of his sternness and Penny picked up the courage to speak to him.

"Stumickosucks," she whispered. "We have come from a long way away to look for you and we have traveled a great deal."

"Yes," interrupted the Indian. "Just like that nice Misterius MacKenzie."

"Is MacKenzie here?" Asked the children in chorus.

"No, I'm sorry, he left a few days ago. He said he had to rush off to solve a mystery in Mexico."

Suddenly something occurred to Alex. "Penny, do you remember what Misterius told us about his ancestor MacKenzie's diary? He told us that a lot of it was damaged, and that many pages were missing. For example, those pages that describe the meeting a few days ago with Stumickosucks!"

"It doesn't matter, young friend. I shall tell you what you want to know."

"Well, for example, we should like to know why you are known as 'the great and sacred secret of the Indians'?"asked Alex, thinking that 'great' was not the adjective that he would have used to describe that little Indian. Stumickosucks seemed to read it in his mind. "Perhaps they should say the most powerful, not the greatest, shouldn't they Alex? No, don't go red, my young friend, there was nothing offensive in your words. I am known in this way because I am a powerful shaman."

"A shaman?" asked the children.

"Forgive us Stumickosucks, but we don't know what a shaman is. Would you like to explain it to us, please?"

"Certainly!"

THE SHAMAN AND THE GREAT SPIRIT

The shaman is a very important figure within the tribe. He is the person who is responsible for maintaining and handing down traditions, legends and magical rituals. He is called both "Man who talks to the Spirits" and 'Medicine Man' because his job is to know all the medicinal herbs and choose the therapy to adopt when a member of the tribe is ill.
The most important of these spirits was the Great Spirit, the creator of the world, called by some tribes "Manitou."
To speak to the Great Spirit, to ask for his protection or thank him for his kindness, Indians have a very important ritual: dancing. The most important ceremony is the Sun Dance, organized by the tribe on the plains before leaving for the hunt.

72

During Indian ceremonies the shaman wears decorated clothes, ritual masks and uses objects rich in symbolic value like the drum. The sound of this instrument allows him to enter the spirit world.

These Sioux hunters are asking for a blessing from the Great Spirit before setting off to go hunting by dancing the Bear Dance.

The Chippewa tribe thanks the Great Spirit for sending the snowfall that have enabled them to move quickly on snow-shoes and easily follow their prey.

STUMICKOSUCKS' DANCE

Our shaman friend has thought up a very special dance for Alex and Penny, different each time it is danced. Do you want to learn to dance with him, all his tribe and your friends?

Watch the dance positions shown by Stumickosucks carefully. Then throw the dice 6 times and, depending to the order of the numbers thrown, decide on the sequence of the positions to do. Turn on the stereo, choose some music that you like and dance the Stumickosucks dance with your friends: enjoy yourselves!

1

2

73

3

4

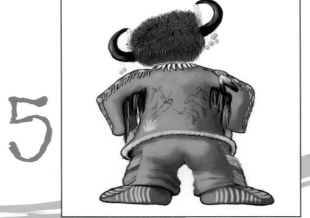

5

6

"Thank you Stumickosucks, now we have understood why you are so important for Indian tribes," said Penny.

"And don't forget, little sister, that we have even solved the mystery! We have carried out our mission!"

"It is now time for you to leave and go home."

"I don't want to leave Pat Hock!" cried Alex trying to hide the big tears that had appeared at the thought of having to leave his four-legged friend.

"Don't worry, Alex, he'll stay with us. You know how we respect Nature, so do not worry. To cheer you up I would like you to take a present with you."

"What present?" asked Alex curiously. "A bow? A sacred drum?"

"No, unfortunately these things would not have the same value in the place you come from. I have made a 'dream-catcher' for you."

"A catcher what?"

"The dream-catcher is a charm that you must hang above the bed. The net it is made with stops bad dreams and lets the nice ones through as these, as everybody knows, are thinner and lighter because they are not weighed down by nasty visions. The feathers on the sides of the net make the good dreams go down to the person sleeping. Put it above your beds and dream of my people."

"Thank you Stumickosucks!" the twins thanked him, moved with emotion. They jumped into the hot-air balloon.

"Goodbye! Goodbye Pat!"

"Neiiiiiiiiiiiiiiiiiiigh!"

STUMICKOSUCKS' DREAM CATCHER

DETACH STUMICOSUCKS' DREAM-CATCHER AND HANG IT ABOVE YOUR BED:
THE NET OF THE INDIAN CHARM WILL CATCH THE NIGHTMARES AND LET ONLY
THE NICE DREAMS THROUGH.

75

SOLUTIONS

PAGE 19

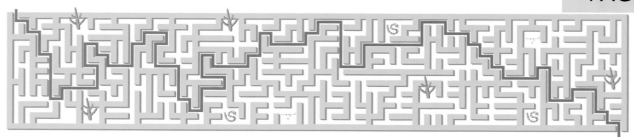

PAGE 19

♣ = 15	♣ − ◎ = ✧	✧ = 10
◎ = 5	✧ + ★ = ❀	❀ = 18
★ = 8	❀ + ✿ = ✳	✳ = 20
✿ = 2	✳ − ★ = ❁	❁ = 12

PAGE 21

THE PIONEER'S TEST

Every correct answer is worth 5 points.
Add up your score, bearing in mind, that all the
statements, even the strangest ones, are TRUE.
If you have reached 20 points, you are a born
pioneer, if you stopped at 15, you still have some
things to learn, but if you have a score
of less than 10, perhaps the hard life of the settler is
not for you!

PAGE 21

T E R A P A R E
H G E T R I I S

THE GREAT PRAIRIES

PAGE 25

10   9
3   6
7   8   5

PAGES 28-29

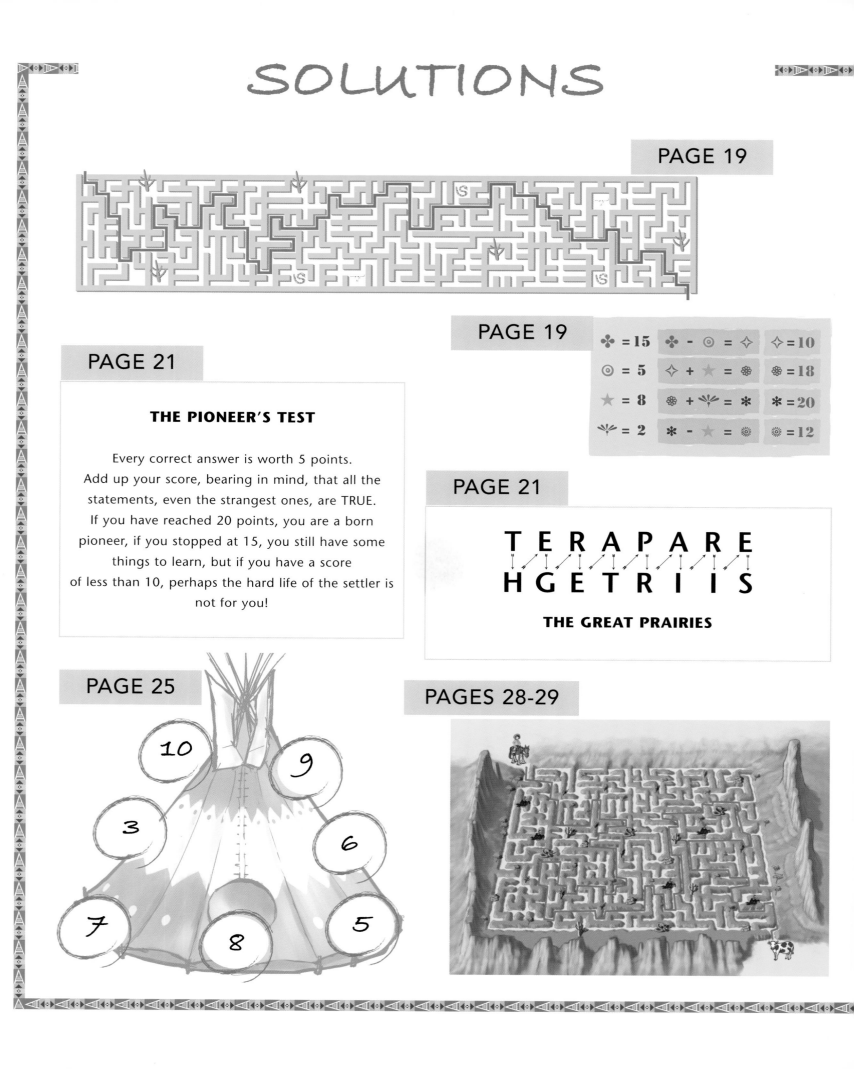

PAGE 33

KKTZKKHZZKEKK
ZCKKOKLZZKKKK
ZZOZKRKKZKKKK
AKKDKKZOKKZRK
KIKVZZZKKEKZRK

THE COLORADO RIVER

PAGE 37

PAGE 37

PAGE 41

**A PUMA
JUMPS FROM
ROCK TO ROCK**

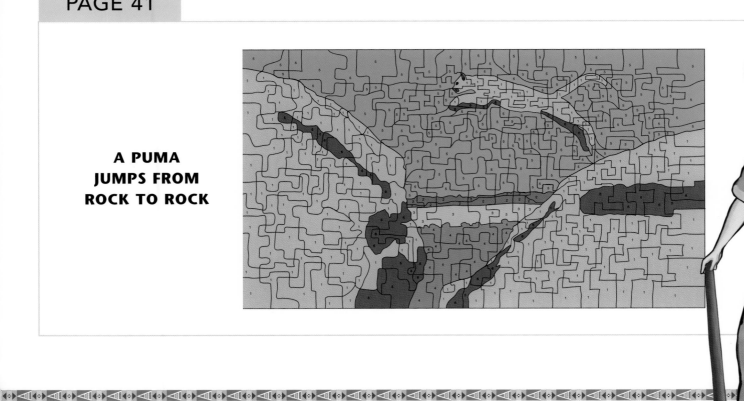

PAGES 42-43

The race is won by the coyote who reaches the end of the track with a lead of six squares over the puma

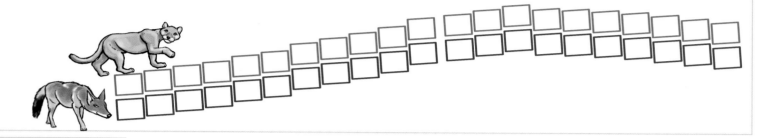

PAGE 43

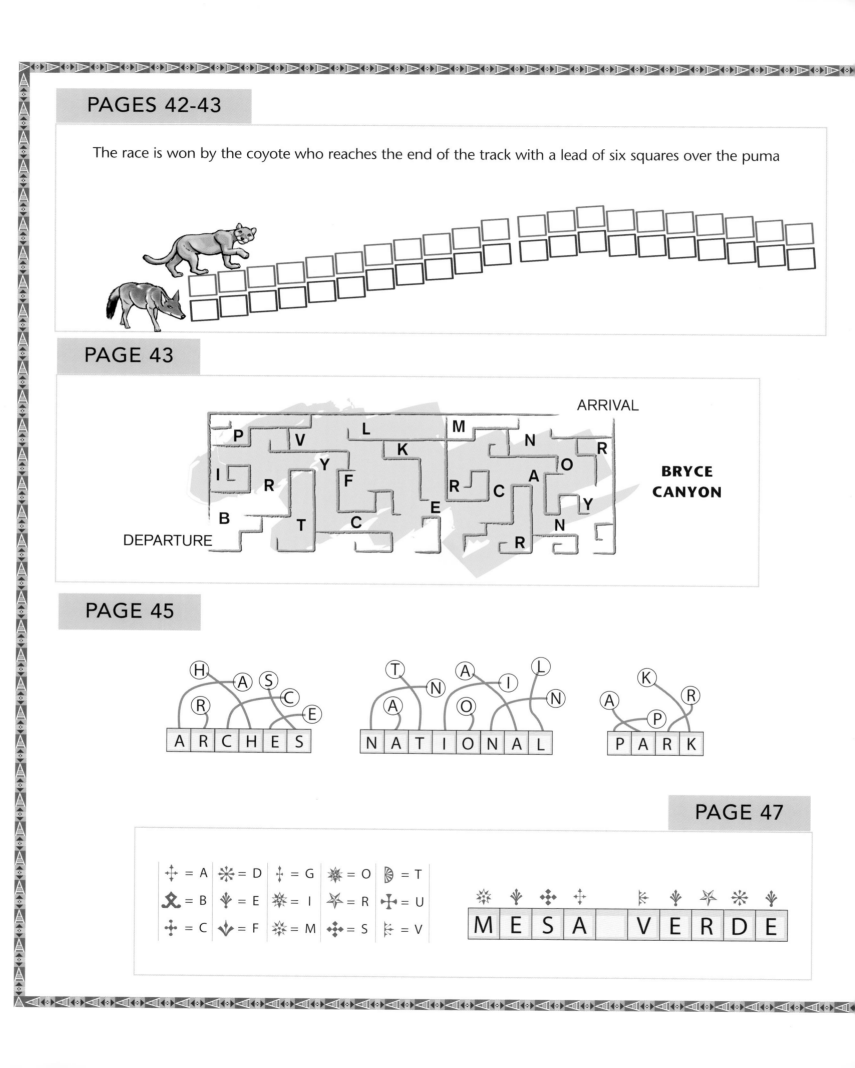

ARRIVAL

DEPARTURE

BRYCE CANYON

PAGE 45

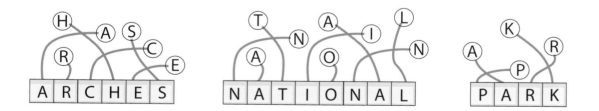

A R C H E S   N A T I O N A L   P A R K

PAGE 47

✛ = A	✳ = D	✚ = G	❈ = O	◗ = T
✖ = B	⚘ = E	✺ = I	✶ = R	✜ = U
✛ = C	⚜ = F	✵ = M	✦ = S	ⴲ = V

M E S A   V E R D E

PAGE 53

MONUMENT VALLEY

PAGE 56

PAGE 61

| B | L | A | C | K | | H | I | L | L | S |

PAGE 65

```
              B¹
      B O B C A T
      I     L
      S     D E E⁵R
      O     E
      N     A³
            E
            A
  G R⁶I Z Z L Y
            E²
```

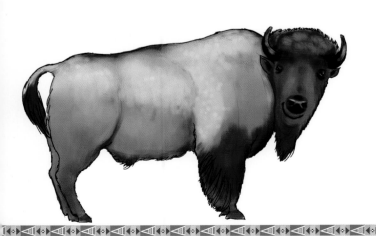

B¹ E² A³ V⁴ E⁵ R⁶

editorial coordination
GIADA FRANCIA

texts
GIADA FRANCIA

graphic designer
PATRIZIA BALOCCO LOVISETTI

artwork
ANGELO COLOMBO

PHOTO CREDITS

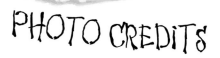

ANTONIO ATTINI/ARCHIVIO WHITE STAR: PAGES 2 (THIRD PHOTO, FOURTH PHOTO), 3 (FIRST PHOTO), 10 CENTER LEFT, 34, 34-35, 38, 38-39, 40, 44, 45, 46, 48, 49, 54-55, 56-57, 62, 63, 64 RIGHT, 66, 67

NATHAN BENN/CORBIS: PAGE 14

JONATHAN BLAIR/CORBIS: PAGE 19 TOP RIGHT

ALAN AND SANDY CAREY: PAGES 3 (SECOND PHOTO), 22-23, 65 BOTTOM RIGHT

BETTMANN/CORBIS: PAGES 19 CENTER, 33, 61 TOP

PRIVATE COLLECTION: PAGE 10 TOP LEFT, 51 TOP LEFT AND RIGHT, 58-59

COLORADO HISTORICAL SOCIETY: PAGE 20 CENTER

CORBIS: PAGES 2 (FIRST PHOTO), 32, 61 CENTER

DANIEL J. COX/CORBIS: PAGES 46-47

INDIPENDENCE NATIONAL HISTORICAL PARK: PAGES 15 BOTTOM RIGHT AND LEFT

JOCELYN ART MUSEUM: PAGE 60 CENTER

LAYNE KENNEDY/CORBIS: PAGE 22

LIBRARY OF CONGRESS, WASHINGTON: PAGE 72 BOTTOM LEFT

MICHAEL & PATRICIA FOGDEN/NATURE PICTURE LIBRARY/CONTRASTO: PAGES 3 (THIRD PHOTO), 64 LEFT

NATIONAL MUSEUM OF AMERICAN ART, DC/ART RESOURCE, NY: PAGES 2 (SECOND PHOTO), 58, 60 TOP, 72 TOP, 72 BOTTOM RIGHT

B. MOOSE PETERSON/ARDEA: PAGE 65 CENTER LEFT

PHOTOSERVICE ELECTA/AKG IMAGES: PAGE 18 TOP, 20 TOP

PAUL A. SOUDERS/CORBIS: PAGE 65 TOP RIGHT

UNDERWOOD PHOTO ARCHIVE: PAGE 36 LEFT AND RIGHT

UTAH HISTORICAL SOCIETY: PAGE 20 BOTTOM

JEFF VANUGA/CORBIS: PAGE 65 CENTER RIGHT

KENNAN WARD/CORBIS: PAGE 65 BOTTOM LEFT

JIM WARK: PAGES 14-15

M. WATSON/ARDEA: PAGE 65 TOP LEFT

© 2007 White Star s.p.a.
Via Candido Sassone, 22/24 - 13100 Vercelli, Italy
www.whitestar.it

Translation: Catherine Howard - Editing: Erin McCloskey

ISBN 978-88-544-0245-4

Reprint: 1 2 3 4 5 6   11 10 09 08 07

Printed in China - Color separation by: Fotomec, Turin, Italy